ARIES

EDITED BY AUSTIN P. SHEEHAN,
MIKHAEYLA KOPIEVSKY & NIKKY LEE

THE ZODIAC SERIES

The Zodiac Series is a collection of twelve speculative fiction anthologies, each focusing on one of the Zodiac signs. The anthologies feature short stories and poems inspired by each sign, and retellings of the various myths behind those signs.

Capricorn Aquarius Pisces

Aries Taurus Gemini

Cancer Leo Virgo

Libra Scorpio Sagittarius

The Zodiac Series has been produced by Aussie Speculative Fiction, and each anthology contains a diverse selection of tales by talented writers from Australia and New Zealand.

I AM ARIES

Zoey Xolton

I am the Ram and my constellation is Aries.

My tarot card is The Emperor; I am a confident leader and challenge seeker.

At my best I am courageous, honest and passionate.

At my worst I am stubborn, impulsive and aggressive.

Energetic and wild, like my element: Fire, mine is a Cardinal sign.

I appreciate comfort, organisation, competition and leadership roles.

However, I dislike stagnation, delays and unchallenging tasks.

I am ruled by Mars, and am guardian to the second day of the week.

My colours are red and orange.

About the Author:

Zoey Xolton is an Australian Speculative Fiction writer, primarily of Dark Fantasy, Paranormal Romance, and Horror. Her works have appeared in over one-hundred themed anthologies, with more due for publication!
She has recently celebrated the release of her debut short story collection 'Darkly Ever After'. You can find further details regarding her many publications on her website: www.zoeyxolton.com!

CONTENTS:

FOREWORD

Sasha Hanton

Represented by a ram, Aries is the first sign of the zodiac. Starting the cycle of the zodiac, the cardinal fire sign imbues those under its patronage with strong leadership qualities. And, whilst the myths around this constellation do not stem from the Greek God Ares, it is little wonder that its ruling planet is Mars, named for Ares' Roman counterpart.

The prominent myth about the constellation begins with King Athamas of Boetia, who was married to the nymph Nephele. King Athamas had twin children with Nephele—a son named Phrixus and a daughter named Helle. Variations of the myth differ as to whether he left Nephele or she died, but either way he remarried.

Athamas' new wife, Ino, was jealous of her step-children, and plotted the demise of the twins. Her scheme involved the failure of crops and a fake message from the Oracle to inform her husband the only solution was to sacrifice Phrixus and Helle. At the last minute, just before they were about to be sacrificed, the twins were saved by a ram with a golden fleece, sent by Zeus. The ram carried them away, but as they crossed a narrow stretch of water between Europe and Asia, Helle lost her grip and fell to her death. The straits are still known as Hellespont, though you may also know them as the Dardanelles. Phrixus stayed safe the entire journey and the ram carried him to Colchis where he gave thanks to Zeus by sacrificing the ram and gifted its fleece to King Aeetes.

Zeus placed the ram into the sky as a constellation in honour of its heroism, and King Aeetes hung the fleece in a grove before charging a dragon to guard it. This is, of course, the origin of the Golden Fleece, which later appears in the myth of Jason and the Argonauts. In some versions of the myth, the ram is called the Golden Ram of Aries and the grove is named the Grove of Aries. Both these titles have one name in common: Aries, which is what the sign came to be known as.

Outside of mythology, this constellation is joined with the fourth card of the Major Arcana of the Tarot, the Emperor. Depicted most often as a wise man sitting upon a throne embellished with rams heads, a crown upon his head, a sceptre in the shape of the Egyptian ankh—also called the Crux Ansata or Cross of Life—in his right hand and a globe in his left. The Emperor is a card of authority, leadership, control, and dominion of thought over emotion. In the reverse, this card takes those traits to an extreme and represents emotional immaturity among other things. All these traits can be found in Aries individuals.

For those born between March 21st and April 19th, Aries is the ruling Sun sign. People under Aries' influence are pioneers and innovators; they can be determined and may sometimes act without thinking things fully through. Born from the first sign, they are considered the baby of the zodiac though they make fierce leaders. With the planet Mars overseeing them, Aries individuals can be charged with a volatile temper, immense courage, and boundless energy.

A powerfully sign imbued with raw energy and heroic levels of courage, the encapsulating stories within this anthology will doubtlessly leave strong impressions.

About the Author:

Sasha Hanton grew up in the tropics of Darwin, Northern Territory. From a young age, she devoured books and iced coffee, both of which she continues to intake on an almost daily basis. Now living on beautiful Bribie Island in Queensland, her time is split between writing and spoiling her puppy Miley.

Sasha, who has a Bachelor of Journalism from Bond University, has dabbled in the journalistic profession but finds fiction far more fascinating. Her first published work The Short Story Press Collection draws on her love for a diverse range of genres and passion for short stories. Coming from a multicultural background (Eurasian) she aspires to make her writing inclusive for people from all walks of life and to bring a unique blend of eastern and western culture to her writing.

Throughout her life, she has been a lover of history and mythology, and at any time will find some way to worm one or the other into her storytelling. When she's not writing or reading she can be found walking her dog and volunteering. You can keep up with her writing over on www.theshortstorypress.wordpress.com

THE ARIETIS SHOWDOWN

Austin P. Sheehan

Captain Renner landed his transport on the edge of Beotia Secondus' sprawling spaceport, his guts writhing with unease. He made it a rule to avoid the Arietes Sector. Under normal circumstances he and his crew would have stayed the hell away. But they were desperate. They'd been saddled with a cargo they could only sell on the black markets, and that meant a trip to Beotia Secondus, the dark heart of the Arietis sector. He unstrapped himself from the pilot's seat and looked at his crew. "We're here. Let's do what we came for and get back as soon as we're done."

Theomantis looked up from the Nav comp. "We aren't going to check out what other goods we can get here?"

Renner shook his head. Theo was a good navigator, but was young and naïve. "We need payment in credits. Whatever you pick up at Beotia has a bad habit of sticking around."

"And no one wants a cargo you can't sell," added Marco, his brown eyes smiling under his mop of sandy hair.

"That's what dragged us out here in the first place," Renner muttered.

Renner had pulled on a black jacket over his grimy grey shipsuit, covering the impact pistol in his shoulder holster. Theo had changed into a grey shirt underneath a navy vest, and carried Paeon, a fearsome twin-barrel blaster that he'd blown all his first month's pay on. All Marco had done to prepare for their mission planetside was wash a layer of dirt off his face. He still wore his stained light brown shipsuit with the sleeves rolled up, exposing the red scars covering his right forearm.

They left the Daroc-class transport amongst a maze of other small transport vessels. She was older than many of them, and her grey and blue paint job stood out against the sleek silver and black that dominated the spaceport. Renner and Marco had been doing simple, clean and mostly legitimate transport runs throughout the Outer Systems for years, with Theomantis joining the crew the previous year. More often than not, jobs that looked simple got messy, and that's how they ended up with twelve frozen bodies in their cargo hold, each in its own steel sarcophagus.

Together Renner and his crew entered the writhing slums of Beotia Secondus, where the most wantonly wretched and vile inhabitants of the Outer Systems congregated. The tightness in his stomach hadn't eased. *This was a mistake.* Renner knew what he had to do. Meet his contact who would point him in the direction of a buyer for the A-grade medical supplies on ice in their cargo bay. Simple. *Nothing's ever that simple—not on Boetia Secondus.*

Marco had been with Renner the last time he was here and knew what to expect. But Theomantis was raw and untried. A skinny lad with a big gun. This was his first time in the Arietis sector, and Renner wished he told Theo to stay on the ship. As Renner watched, Theo's eyes darted around and he gripped his sleek twin-barrel blaster tightly.

"He'll be right," Marco said, as if he'd read Renner's mind. "The kid's ready. Hell, if he's scared, it shows he's got more damn sense than us."

Ready or not, Renner couldn't deny that Theo's intimidating weapon could come in handy in a place like this. "Listen," he said, falling into step with Theo. "This is a rough district."

"I know. I can handle myself." Theo held Renner's gaze for a moment before darting back to the slums.

"Just follow my lead," Renner said. "The main thing that marks a person out as someone who doesn't belong is being on edge, being nervous. Stay calm. That's all you gotta do."

Down a lane, hidden from the thrill seekers and the morbidly curious, was the Lilium. A bar Renner knew. The proprietor was a man he had dealt with before, and the only man is the Arietis Sector he trusted.

At the door was a hulking leather-clad monstrosity. *Security.* In Beotia Secondus, the security out front was always for show. Their role was to alert the rest of the staff if the Arietis Police arrived, and to stop people who didn't belong from getting inside. If you didn't know enough to ignore their presence, you didn't belong.

As they passed the guard, one thought crossed Renner's mind. *Hardwired.* He banished it almost immediately—robotic implants had been outlawed for decades, but rumours frequently surfaced throughout the Outer Systems that in the darkest part of the Arietis underworld, people still got hardwired. Renner always dismissed it as nonsense, old spacefarer's tales. Even here, on a planet full of scum, that was the one rule no one would be crazy enough to break.

The Lilium, with its high ceiling supported by a row of thick steel pillars, was just like how Renner remembered it: full of smoke, dimly lit, and covered with the delicate cassolette of sweat, stale beer, tobacco and hopelessness. He made his way to an empty booth, taking note of the other patrons. Hard, foul and sleazy men discussing business. Two men were behind the bar, one's bald head was covered in tattoos, the other had a long beard, streaked with crimson. With their cruel eyes and muscular frames, they weren't there to provide hospitality.

"What'll it be, gentlemen?" asked a woman who couldn't be much older than twenty. Dark wavy red hair spilled down her bare shoulders, a tight silver strip of fabric covered her chest, half-concealing the swirl of a black and red tattoo.

"We're here to see Billdog."

"Business then. Well, that's too bad."

"Why's that?"

She softened her voice a fraction. "First, Billdog isn't here, and second, it's been a slow day."

Shit.

"What do you mean Billdog isn't here?"

She held Renner's gaze for a moment. "I guess you haven't been out this way for a while. Take a seat, I'll bring over some drinks and fill you in."

They found an empty booth, the floor under their boots crunched with broken glass.

Theo rested his hand on the grip of his blaster, eyes shifting around the room.

"I don't like the feel of this," Marco said, his voice low.

Renner shook his head. "Me neither. This place has sure changed if they've got girls turning tricks." His eyes now adjusted to the light, he saw women—all wearing forced smiles—sat at the tables or the bar.

"Here we are." The redhead smiled and slid into the booth with practiced ease, placing three full glasses on the table. "I'm Violantia, but just call me Vio."

Renner sipped the beer, feigning nonchalance, trying to detect any hint that liquid was laced with poison or drugs. It seemed clean, if not a little weak. "I'm Captain Renner."

Vio nodded and keyed a code at the edge of the table and a low hum surrounded the booth.

"What are you doing?" Marco asked, one of his gloved hands on the table, the other reaching for the blaster around his waist.

"Sorting out privacy while we negotiate," Vio said. "With this screen up, we won't be overheard."

"Negotiate what?" Theomantis asked.

"In this place, you're either here for business or pleasure. Your business was with Billdog." She turned to Renner, compassion in her eyes. "He's . . . well he's underground. He can't help you anymore."

Shit. Renner took a drink of his beer, thinking of his friend. Vio watched, no doubt trying to work out how close he and Billdog had been. He had to be careful, he had trusted Billdog, and trustworthy people on Beotia were rare as habitable comets.

"Who runs this place now, then?" Theo asked.

"Inos."

"The King of Beotia," Marco whispered under his breath. "Fuck."

Renner's stomach fell. Billdog was dead, and Inos' reputation as a depraved butcher had travelled through the Outer Rim. It inspired one thing in Renner. Fear. "We're leaving," he said, making a move to get up. *If you work with Inos, you either end up working for him, or you end up dead.*

"Wait," Vio pleaded. "I knew Billdog. I might be able to help—if you can help me."

"We get it. We're leaving."

"And we're being watched." A warning in her voice.

Renner looked into her eyes. Honest. "Okay. We'll drink our beers. You tell what you're offering. And then we'll leave."

"Billdog trusted me. I know some of his contacts. I might be able to get you to them."

Marco leaned in, resting his elbows on the table. "What would you want from us?"

Dammit, Marco. Don't show her we're eager.

Vio shot a meaningful look at the exit. "Get me out," she whispered.

"You can't leave?" Renner asked.

She shook her head.

It was worse than he thought. His contact dead. Inos had turned the Lilium into a brothel and the girls were his prisoners. Renner's thoughts drifted to the security guard out front. Leaving here would not be easy. Then another thought. *Could he trust Vio?* He had no way to know if her story was true. But why would she lie? The only thing he was sure about was that coming here had been a mistake.

Renner took another swig of his beer, weighing up his options. Running a transport through the black heavens was always a risk. Everything was a gamble. They'd taken a risk coming here, and so far it hadn't panned out. But returning to his ship, getting off-planet and never coming back, that was a gamble too. Either he was going to get out of this with a contact to sell his cargo to, covering the cost of much-needed repairs, or he was going to get out of here with a cargo he would have to jettison, and hope to pick up a simple job wherever they went next. And then there was the possibility of not getting out at all.

Marco sipped his beer and grimaced, then ran the cool glass against his scarred forearm. "Tastes like what I wash the reclamation system out with, but at least it's cold."

Theo took his hand off the Paeon and began shuffling a deck of cards.

Smart kid. Renner glanced around the room. At the women. At the bruises behind their make-up. At their missing teeth. Then he looked at Violantia. There was a spark to her. A promise. A potential. Inos wouldn't want to let her go. To let any of them go. "Alright, Vio. If you want us to help you, we need to know who you are."

Theo dealt out a hand.

"I used to crew the Baran, a transport out of the Algieba system." Vio was speaking slowly, her voice low, as she scanned the cards in her hand. "Luder was our captain. He brought us here trying to make some fast money, but the deal went bad. He ended owing the wrong people and couldn't pay up. Billdog took me in, gave me a job. I almost saved enough for a ticket out of here . . ."

"Why didn't you just get a job on another transport?" Theo asked, watching as a woman escorted two men down a stairwell.

"Because no self-respecting captain would hire from a place like this. Not if they didn't want trouble." Vio glanced at Renner over the top of her cards.

Renner nodded. No way would he employ anyone with Beotia Secondus on their resume.

"What happened to Billdog?" Marco asked in a whisper as he placed two cards on the table.

"He ended up owing Inos." Vio's voice was a bitter whisper.

Renner shook his head. He knew his friend. Knew he hadn't wanted anything to do with the likes of Inos. "The Dog would never have got involved," he countered.

"Inos has his hands in every pie on this planet. If you stick around long enough, you get involved."

Renner took another look around the Lilium while they played out the hand. You weren't going to find anyone who wasn't a sadistic fuck on this planet, let alone in a bar owned by a brutal criminal kingpin. *Shit.* Leaving Vio in Inos' hands was going to be a tough decision, but he didn't come here to get involved in other people's business.

Vio continued her story as Theo shuffled the cards for another round. "About six months back Inos and his goons came in and shot the place to hell. He only let the women live. He branded us." She flicked her hair to the side, letting Renner see a steel clasp gripped to her ear, held in place by thick screws. Then, pulling her silver top down, she revealed a tattoo of a bold black 'I' poking out from a red and gold crown on her breast. "He let his arsehole buddies Tonny and Valdemar have their way with us." She glanced at the men behind the bar, her voice dark and full of hate. "Getting out of this bar isn't going to be good enough. I have to get off this rock. That tattoo marks me as Inos' possession, and he's got long arms."

Renner went to the bathroom and considered Violantia's plight. It stank. The floors hadn't been cleaned in years, unidentifiable slime pools congealed on the floor, somewhere between vomit and excrement. He grimaced. *Some things haven't changed.*

Washing his hands, Renner had almost made up his mind to help Vio. They still needed a buyer for his cargo, maybe she could help him find one. He'd go back to the ship with his crew and come up with a plan. Regardless, she deserved better than being Inos' slave.

"Haven't seen you 'round here before." A man emerged from the darkness and stood next to Renner.

Renner grunted, glancing at the man in the mirror, but could only see tattoos and dark hair.

"What are you here for then, business or pleasure?"

"I came here looking for the Dog," Renner said, wanting confirmation of Vio's story.

"If you knew anything, you'd know the Dog don't work here no more. But wasn't you just settling in with that red-haired whore?"

Renner's blood turned to ice. He had made a mistake. "When I heard the Dog wasn't around, I thought maybe a little pleasure wouldn't be so bad."

"So your business was good enough for the Dog, but not good enough for Inos? He ain't going to like hearing that."

"Don't tell him then." Renner did up his pants and turned to face the man. A tattoo similar to Vio's was front and centre on his throat.

The man smiled, a threatening grin revealing sharp teeth. "We are businessmen. Call me Tonny. You came here for business, and Inos has a policy of not letting a partner leave without making a deal."

"Inos is not here though, is he?"

"No, but I can make deals on his behalf. Do not worry. So, what is your business?"

"I have bodies in my cargo hold. Twelve of them. Billdog used to hook me up with someone I could sell them to."

"This does not interest Inos." Tonny drew an impact pistol from his holster, aiming it at Renner. "If he wants body, boom—" Tonny gestured with the weapon, "—he gets body. Very simple. Very easy."

Renner gritted his teeth. The bodies he had were black market medical goods, A-grade raw materials that organs and blood could be harvested from. Dealing with Inos himself would have been easier than this mercenary, though neither of them seemed to care about keeping other people alive. One thought flashed through his mind. *If you do a deal with Inos, you end up owing Inos. If you owe Inos, you end up dead.*

"You must have something else you can trade. Your crew?" A glint in his eye. "Your ship, perhaps?"

A threat to take his ship. A threat that Renner could only ever meet with violence. "Not in this lifetime." Renner thrust forward, shoving against Tonny, pushing him backwards.

Tonny struck down with the butt of his pistol. As he stepped backwards to absorb Renner's blow, his foot slipped in a pool of dark slime and he fell to his knees.

Renner continued his forward momentum, driving his knee into Tonny's face, throwing his head back against the steel door frame with a heavy thunk.

Tonny was out cold.

Renner pushed into the bar room of the Lilium, his heart racing. "Marco, Theo, time to go!" he shouted.

The bartenders glanced at each other, ducked down and came back up brandishing weapons. Behind them, the security cameras showed Tonny unconscious on the bathroom floor. *Shit.* The bald-headed man gripped two massive blaster pistols, one in each hand. The bearded man swung a white-hot laser axe. "Stay right there!" The command echoed through the room.

Marco, Theo and Vio jumped behind the booth as Renner reached for his blaster.

The bartender fired a round, and the booth exploded in a shower of red and white cards.

Renner fired back from behind a steel pillar, his heart racing.

Marco darted behind another booth as Vio threw a glass of beer, smashing the man with the axe in the face.

"Come here, you red-haired bitch!" he yelled, jumping over the bar.

Vio stepped forward to face him, defiance in her eyes and a bar stool in her hands. "Come get me, Valdemar," she growled.

Under fire from the other bartender, the air electric with the bursts of blaster fire, Renner shot wildly into the chaos.

As people fled through the exit, Theo aimed both barrels of the Paeon at the pistol-wielding bartender. In a deafening blast, the bartender's arm was blown off. Slick, glistening steel lay exposed below his shoulder.

Renner's heart stopped. A cybernetic arm. *Shit.*

Theo froze, his mouth agape.

Vio's bar stool lay in pieces at her feet. She'd evaded the laser axe so far, and Valdemar's bloody face was furious. She was going to get herself killed.

The one-armed bartender glanced at the shower of sparks where his right arm used to be, smiled, and levelled his hand-held cannon at Theo.

Renner aimed his blaster at the hardwired bartender and squeezed the trigger. Nothing happened. The weapon was dead in his hands. *Shit.* Renner watched helplessly as the bartender fired, as

Theo's chest exploded, and blood, gore and shards of bone spattered across the wall behind him. *Shit.*

Marco fired at the cybernetic bartender, half his face covered in Theo's blood. He hit nothing but bottle after bottle of liquor, spraying the bar with glass and alcohol.

Violantia was still evading blow after blow from Valdemar's axe, throwing whatever was in reach at her attacker. By some miracle she'd beaten the axe's lethal edge so far, but her luck couldn't last much longer.

Renner ducked into a nearby stairwell to change angles and reload, so he could fire at Valdemar without taking Marco or Vio out.

Behind Marco, the massive frame of the security guard filled the doorway. He scanned the scene, face impassive. Panicked men rushed past, some covered in blood, but the guard just stood there, serene.

Renner's hands trembled as he ejected the spent charge clip from his blaster and patted down his pockets for a replacement. His blood turned to ice. He was out. *Oh no.* He scanned the Lilium looking for another weapon when he saw a lone figure at the far end of the bar. One of Inos' women.

Her slim arm, trembling, drew a cigar from the cabinet. She lit it, and when the tip was smoking, looked from Vio to Renner, as if asking a question.

Renner nodded.

She smiled and flicked the cigar behind the bar.

The cheap booze covering the floor ignited, and the hardwired bartender screamed as the fire engulfed him.

Valdemar paused as the hideous screams echoed through the bar, but not Vio. She kicked his right hand, loosening his grip on the axe, then she followed through with a punch to his face. As he staggered backwards, he dropped the axe and drew a blaster pistol from the waistband of his pants. "Let's see you evade this, bitch."

"Let's see you fuck off!" Marco shouted, then pulled the trigger on Theo's double-barrel blaster.

The bartender's body was thrown into the roaring fire by Paeon's fury.

"Marco—behind you!" Renner shouted as the leather-clad security guard stepped into the room.

As the guard lifted his arm, a chaingun emerged from his leather sleeve. *Another hardwired freak.* Marco and Vio dived out of the way as death screamed down those barrels, right into the chest of the woman at the bar. When Renner looked back, she was nothing but a steaming pile of meat.

Vio threw an ashtray at the guard. It bounced off his head and fell to the ground.

As the leather-clad guard fired the chaingun in Vio's direction, Marco ducked behind a pillar, moments before the booth he'd taken cover behind burst into flames.

Coughing from the smoke, desperate for a way out, Renner leaped towards the inferno, grabbing the handle of Valdemar's discarded axe and taking cover. The heat of the fire was overwhelming. He had to move. Staggering to his feet, Renner jumped behind a pillar a fraction of a second before the booth he'd hid behind disappeared under blast after blast of the chaingun.

The fire was spreading, racing towards the door, filling the Lilium with smoke. They had to get past the guard. Vio was pinned down by the continuous barrage from the chaingun.

Renner had one roll of the dice left. "Take a shot, Marco, I'm out!" he shouted, hoping to be heard over the thunder.

"I can hardly fucking see," Marco shouted back.

"Just do it!"

A thunderous blast deafened Renner. With his eyes stinging from the smoke, he peered past the pillar. The hulking shape of the guard still blocked the exit. Marco had missed.

The guard swung his chaingun towards Marco as Renner stepped out from behind the pillar, the laser axe in his hand. He lunged forward and threw the axe with all his strength at the security guard.

It split his skull open.

It split the top half of his body open.

Marco was first to the door, with Renner and Vio close behind.

"Let's get the fuck out of here," Marco said between harsh coughs.

Renner glanced back in time to see the raging fire claim Theo's lifeless body. *We never should never have come.*

Violantia grunted as she pulled the axe from the guard's steaming body. "I know a place."

"No—we have to get into the black heavens," said Renner. "Inos will tear this colony apart looking for us. No matter how safe your place is, it isn't going to be safe enough."

"He'll come after your ship."

"If we don't get off the planet now, we never will."

Distant sirens droned as they emerged from the smoke-filled alley into the grimy neon streets of Beotia Secondus.

Renner slid his spent blaster into its holster and pushed out into the crowd, Marco and Vio followed. They needed to hurry, to get to the spaceport as soon as possible, but Vio grabbed Renner's arm and dragged him down another alley. "I have to get my tag off, or they'll track us." She held the laser axe close to her face. The illumination of the white-hot blade lit up the steel attached to her ear.

"You can't be serious . . ." Marco said.

"It's a tracking device. It's the only way." She turned to Renner, holding the handle of the axe out to him. "Just make it quick." Vio's trembling hand reached for Marco's under the illumination of the alleyway's neon lights.

The axe was heavy in Renner's hand. If he didn't remove the tag, Inos could follow her wherever she went. And he didn't have the time or the tools to do a delicate job. He had to do this.

Vio gasped as the laser's edge bit into her ear, tears welling in her eyes, but she clenched her jaw, her hands squeezing Marco's like a vice.

Renner kept his hand as still as possible while the scent of burning flesh and singed hair filled the alley. The tag—and most of Vio's ear—fell to the wet mud with a thunk.

They emerged from the alley into the filthy, crowded streets near the spaceport as a light rain began to fall. Massive figures loomed at the corners. Cruel eyes followed their movements. Was that one of Inos' men? Was that one of his tattoos?

Renner's legs ached. His lungs burned. Sitting in the captain's chair was not good preparation for running through the sewers of the universe. They stopped at the edge of the spaceport, exhausted, weak and covered in sweat.

Marco gasped deep, ragged breaths. His grey shipsuit now stained red with the blood of their crewmate. "Captain," he panted. "With all goddamn respect, I'm going to mutiny if you ever mention coming back here."

"There are no guarantees in the black heavens, Marco. But you have my word that I won't set course for this hellhole again." Renner turned to Vio. "Now let's get off this damned rock."

Under cover of rain, they traversed the spaceport and made their way back to their ship.

"Welcome to the *Persephone*," Renner said as he opened the cargo bay doors for Violantia. They'd at least get her out of Inos' reach. *And then what?*

She smiled and stepped past him into the shadows of the *'Seph's* cargo bay, followed by Marco.

Turning back to look out over the sprawling colony for the last time, the spaceport's neon yellow lights reflected off his wet jacket. For a moment, he was golden.

As Renner entered the ship, the strain in his chest eased. He was home. "Marco, prep the *'Seph* for immediate launch, and suit up. Set the cargo bay's outer airlock to detonate on my command."

Marco turned towards the engineering bay without even pausing to wipe the blood off his face.

"Where do you want me, Captain?" Violantia's silver top and skin was covered in blood, sweat and ash.

"Follow me." Renner led her past the twelve heavy steel boxes and up the stairs to the catwalk above the cargo bay. "Have you been on a Daroc-class before?"

"No." Vio shook her head, taking in the dull grey walls, the rope netting, and the ATV secured in the corner. "But I'm a quick learner."

Renner opened the door separating the cargo bay from the rest of the ship and stepped through into a narrow hallway. "That was the cargo bay, the bridge is at the end of the hall, crew's mess and galley to the right, medbay to the left."

As they entered the bridge, the intercom lit up with an incoming transmission from Marco in the engineering bay. "Captain, she's ready for launch. Give me a moment to get into my suit and strap down."

"You've got twenty seconds."

"Why did you tell him to get into his suit?" A note of fear crept into Vio's voice.

Renner pulled out the emergency EVA suit from below the pilot's chair. "Because I don't want him to die."

Vio nodded apprehensively. "Where can I sit?"

Renner's eyes fell on the empty chair at the Nav console and a surge of guilt and pain rose inside him. "Strap yourself in at the Comms console. All other seats are taken." Renner turned away from Theo's chair and wiped his eyes before pulling on his emergency EVA suit over his clothes. As soon as he was suited up, he toggled the intercom. "Beotia Control, this is the *Persephone* announcing our departure."

"Travel well, Captain Renner." A cold, slimy voice emerged from the intercom, and a spear of ice shot up Renner's spine. "I trust your pleasure was to your satisfaction?"

Vio froze. "That's Inos," she said, her face ashen. "What are we going to do? He won't let us leave . . ."

"You get into that EVA suit. Marco and I'll get us out of here." Renner reached for the headset and adjusted the microphone. "The company was grand, but the fireproofing needs work." Renner started up the thrusters and then toggled the intercom. "Marco, are you ready?"

"Just strapping down now."

"Good. As soon as the launch thrusters cut out, get the airlock loaded with our cargo."

"Understood, Captain."

"What are you planning, Renner?" Vio asked, strapping herself into the Comms chair. "You can't beat Inos. He's won. From the moment you walked into his bar, he'd won. I was a goddamned idiot to think I'd ever get out."

"Vio, I don't know how long you spent planetside, but the rules are different in the black heavens. If we can take off, we've got a chance." As Renner spoke, he initiated the *Persephone's* launch sequence. "And look, even if we are doomed, Marco and I have been travelling the abyss as long as we've been alive." Renner raised his voice to be heard over the while of the thrusters kicking in. "If we're going to die, we're going to die up there." Renner thought of Theo, wishing he could have spared him. Wishing he could have saved him.

Vio nodded. "Is there anything I can do?"

Renner shook his head as the *'Seph* launched. The bridge shook with the force of the engines, the thunder of the launch thrusters blasting them up above the city. Vio and Renner were pushed back into their chairs by the sudden g-forces. Straining against the power of the launch, Renner cut the launch thrusters. They were still well in the Beotian atmosphere. He gave her just enough thrust to fight against the planet's gravity and slowly gain altitude, while typing the command to increase the pressure inside the ship.

"Why a slow launch?" Vio asked. "Don't we want to get the hell out of here and get our shields up?"

Before Renner could answer, the comms display lit up with another transmission.

"Open the channel, Vio."

She nodded and flicked the switch.

Inos' growl filled the bridge. "Don't think I'm going to let you out of here, not when you've got something that belongs to me. My friend Tonny—you remember Tonny?—he's on his way to pay you a visit."

Vio brought up the short-range scan. Another ship had launched. She brought up the ship's ID. The *Starthasher*. It was on their tail and closing fast.

Renner clenched his teeth as the *'Seph* shook beneath him. His fingers itched for the switch to activate the shields, but activating shields in-atmosphere would have him blacklisted in all colony planets. A shielded ship crashing into a colony would cause massive devastation. Renner grinned, *it would probably improve Beotia Secondus, though.*

He looked out the viewscreen at the pale grey mountains below them and reached for the intercom. "Marco, are you ready?"

"Just about, Captain. Cargo bay loaded."

"Get yourself tied down pronto."

Renner cut thrust, his brow beading with sweat. This was the moment his plan depended on. He toggled the comms system to open all channels and sent out a distress call. "Mayday, mayday. This is the transport *Persephone* in need of assistance. We've had a system malfunction. Main thrusters off-line. Cabin pressure dropping."

The display showed that cabin pressure was nearly four times the pressure outside, and Vio looked to Renner, confusion and fear in her eyes. The other screen showed the pursuing shuttle directly behind them, the *'Seph* well within range of her guns.

"This is the *Starthrasher*." Tonny's voice echoed through the cabin. "Sorry to hear about your troubles, but they will be all over quick. No shields. One shot. Dead. Very easy."

"Don't shoot, Tonny, we're defenceless!" Renner pleaded as he pressed the button to open the cargo bay's inner airlock.

"No. You hurt my friends. You kill Inos' people. You take his women. You make me, Tonny, look like numbskull. So you do this, Renner. You make me do this."

Renner toggled the ship-wide intercom. "Hold on tight, Marco!" he shouted, then hit the detonator.

The *Persephone* shook as the outer airlock disintegrated. Renner and Vio were thrown back and forth in their seats as the pressure dropped and alarms lit up the bridge, the claxons drowned out by the deafening blast.

Twelve steel containers exploded out of the airlock, the force of the cargo bay depressurising sent them shooting, torpedo-like, away from the *Persephone*.

And straight into the *Starthrasher*.

Without shields, the pursuing vessel was torn apart as the deadly cargo ripped through it, and winked off the *Persephone's* radar.

Renner shut the inner airlock, and one of the blaring alarms cut out. The display screen indicated pressure slowly returning to the ship.

Vio reached for the intercom. "Are you all right back there Marco?"

"I'm here." His voice was weak. "I'm here."

Renner's heart lifted. "We got the bastards, Marco. Now come to the bridge."

"Will do, Captain. Just give me a moment."

Renner engaged the *'Seph'*s main thrusters and set her on a course to Algieba.

"What now?" Vio took off her emergency EVA suit and looked up at Renner from under her wavy red hair.

"We burn hard for Algieba, and never come back."

"And after that?" she asked, eyes bright with defiance. "Are you just going to dump me there?"

Renner softened his tone and looked into her eyes. "I don't know. And I'm not even going to think about it until the Arietis sector is light years behind us—until I know we're safe."

She nodded. "I understand. Thank you for getting me out of there. For everything . . ."

Marco entered the bridge, his wide grin fading as his eyes fell on Theo's empty chair. "I can't believe that worked, Captain!"

"Me either." Renner stood and embraced Marco. "You did good."

"But I'm more surprised we got rid of that damn cargo," Marco said with a laugh.

Vio grinned. "I told you I knew a guy."

Renner smiled at her. "You did great, you both did. But we're not in the clear yet. We need to burn as hard as we can for Algieba, and we need to do it before they send someone else on our tail. Marco, I need you to run some system checks, see how much thrust the *'Seph* can take."

Marco strapped himself into the chair at the Engineering console and brought up the system diagnostics. "She's responding well, Captain. Inner airlock at full strength, hull integrity stable, all thrusters in order. She should be able to handle a full burn."

"All right, let's do it." Before increasing thrust, Renner glanced at the empty chair where Theo used to sit. *Should be sitting.* They would mourn their crewmate once they were safe. He glanced at the Comms chair. Vio had been through hell. While it had scarred her, it hadn't beaten her. She was smart, she was strong, and with the black heavens full of scumbags, you'd be a fool to be trusting. Renner smiled to himself. *Whatever you pick up at Beotia has a bad habit of sticking around.*

About the Author:

Austin grew up in Victoria's high country, and despite living in Melbourne for ten years, still feels at home amongst the mountains. You'll often find mountains in his stories, whether they are science fiction, fantasy, alternative history or horror. To discover what secrets are hidden in the mountains, go to www.austinpsheehan.com or find him on twitter @AustinPSheehan.

WAR MACHINE

Amanda McLeod

The shells were an endless deathly metal hail. We cowered in the trenches, focused solely on staying alive. Only Captain Ramsay was enjoying himself. The stink of dying men, the salty-metallic tang of blood in the air stirred him. His eyes bulged in his reddened face as he stalked the muddy pits, barking orders, giving short but impassioned speeches, trying to inspire in us his same thirst for victory at any price.

Some of the men revered Captain Ramsey, others thought he was possessed. There had been rumours flying about questionable treatment of prisoners—which didn't surprise me—but there was also talk of strange shadows cast on the walls of his tent late at night, from the lamps within. That sort of rubbish I had no time for; I was too busy trying to stay alive. The man might be deranged, but in my mind there was no doubt—he was a war machine.

"Come on, you useless, slack-jawed fools!" he screamed, spittle flying from his lips, sticking to his beard. "That gate is ours! Let us take back what was stolen from us!" Mania had taken him. "Second division! You'll attack the western flank!" He gestured wildly at the fortifications. "Fifth! You're to fire heavily on the eastern towers!" His eyes glowed like the devil's own. "First division, through the centre." His breath was ragged with fury. "Like a battering ram from the gates of hell itself."

We shifted, chewing our nails. Ramsay's bloodlust was unsettling. He'd throw us all in front of enemy guns without a second thought if it meant he'd emerge victorious. I knew he was a good leader, but that didn't mean I wanted to die for him.

"Ready yourselves!" he barked, and strode off to oversee preparations for the Second and Fifth.

"He's lost it," muttered Fitzgerald. "Can't see two feet in front of his own face. This is madness, but if it works, he'll take all the glory."

"I dunno," I replied. "He's made Captain—he wouldn't still be alive if some of his lunatic ideas weren't actually good."

"Bootlicker." Fitzgerald's voice was dark.

"Not likely. No way do I want that kind of responsibility. I'm just saying you don't get pegged for leadership without doing some kind of, you know, leading."

"Oh he's leading, all right. Leading us to our deaths." A high pitched whistling sound followed the bullet as it lodged in the wall of the trench behind us. We dropped, face down in the sludge, trying to keep breathing. Fear chewed at my insides. I fought not to add my own vomit to the mix.

Ramsay reappeared, bellowing, stomping his feet, snorting at the scent of battle. The very air seemed to glow red around him. Was I mistaken, or was he . . . bigger?

"First! Fall in! Prepare for the final offensive!" he bellowed, haranguing us into formation with razor-sharp focus. Before I could think, we were surging forward, Ramsay's "Charge!" hanging in the air like gunsmoke. I could still hear the madman yelling at us as we ran towards the enemy and our own certain ends, and a scream escaped my own throat as battle rage overtook me.

I caught a glimpse of Ramsay, stalking back and forth, waving his bayonet. He was eight feet tall, bearded and burly, wearing . . . a helmet? My eyes must have been bleary with ash and gunpowder, or exhaustion had me hallucinating. He was covered in blood, bellowing at the sky, his face split with a smile of sick glee. The hairs stood up on the back of my neck. The men who revered Ramsey, were they right? Was it possible he was more than human, somehow?

We struggled on, amid blood spatters and limbs and corpses. Around me, strong men screamed for their mothers as they lay dying in ways beyond their nightmares. The shrieking bullets, the wet thwacks as they found their marks, the stink of shit as we voided our bowels in death or fear. Only base instinct stood between us and them. We surged forward in one final wave of smoke, confusion, and fury.

The day was ours. We fought like men possessed, driving the enemy back and retaking the gate. Around me, men fell like trees. Ramsay's triumph was costly.

In the confusion after I found Fitzgerald in the mud, his intestines spilling from his stomach, felled as the enemy retreated.

"Where's our fearless leader then?" he gasped.

I laughed through tears. "Stalked behind the lines like the mad bastard he is. Sent us out to win a glorious victory in his name, then headed to the command tent to plot his next move. Probably tucked up in his canvas temple now, while the other captains worship at his feet."

"Ha," panted Fitzgerald, his last word cut short. "Typical Ram—"

About the Author:

Amanda McLeod is an author and artist based in Canberra. Her poetry and fiction have appeared in many places, both in print and online. She's also the Managing Editor of Animal Heart Press. When she's not immersed in words, she's enjoying a good coffee or out and about with her dogs. Rainy days are her favourites. Find out more at amandamcleodwrites.com

THE SUBJUGATION OF RAMA

Jenna Whittaker

1101 BC

"Kill me," she whispered, eyes closed.

"No, I . . . I can't."

"She told you to, Carulis." Annaya looked up, hazel eyes shimmering with unshed tears. She sat down in the snow, heedless as it soaked her green velvet dress. "Our Queen told you to."

His hands shook. He'd followed Queen Kepi his entire life as a loyal servant and guard—as had they all, in their own ways. Yet now the Queen had commanded him to kill so many who had stood by her as she'd grown from a small child; people who'd been by her side for decades. People like Annaya.

Mahomet had brought this madness.

1100 BC

It was the eve of the rule Rama, the horned one. She was once the heralder of spring, of new life, the moment of vernal equinox. To become the sum of all things, she had to know all things—not just life, but death.

Mahomet was the heralder of the blight.

"You should not create me," the statue hissed, her sibilant voice echoing around the chamber. "I will die when the spring comes. Rama brings spring, life, and with it, I will die," she warned.

"So also will we." The twenty girls stepped out of the darkness, lit only by the red earrings glowing like halos around their faces. In reverent silence, they filed in.

"If spring comes, we all die. Mahomet, wake, and let spring never come." As one, they let their blood, dragging the ceremonial knives down their forearms, dripping ochre running into the maze of channels in the floor, winding their way to the statue of Mahomet.

Her statue drank, and Mahomet woke. The statue's eyes flashed red, and the room rumbled around them. Dust filtered through the air, cracks opening up in the ceiling; sunlight pouring into the darkness. The girls backed away, coughing; covering their eyes from the blinding light, before they turned and ran.

The tower of stairs wound round and round, rising up from the depths of the ground to the surface, and it seemed to take hours to scale. The darkness was absolute; stumbling up every step, escaping the crumbling stone below; it was a race for their life. The girls gasped breath, muscles burning, and collapsed onto the grass as soon as they reached it.

One by one they rose to their feet, trembling, clinging to each other as they turned back to look behind them. Nothing followed, but the rumbling continued beneath their feet.

Then it stopped.

The ground sunk in on itself, a massive crater into the darkness below, dragging in the trees, the grass; and the red-robed girls.

The blight entered the land.

1101 BC

Carulis glanced round, heart pounding in his chest. Thunder rumbled in the distance, and it sent chills down his spine, despite the cold surrounding him, and the furs and leathers he wrapped tight around himself. He gripped his knife with numb fingers.

Annaya gasped, but didn't move from her position in the snow. They both knew what those noises were.

Shadow walkers. Beasts. Monsters that Mahomet had summoned when she'd risen. Giant, hulking creatures, void of any features or detail; just black shapes, so tall they towered over the trees. She'd used them to protect herself and Queen Kepi during the first riots, but now the goat-demon had no use for them.

And so they walked. Aimlessly roaming, silent but for their thundering footsteps.

To see one was death.

"Just do it now," Annaya begged him. "You can't return without my blood on your hands; she won't let you live. Please, Carulis. There's no hope left for any of us."

It wasn't right. Carulis groaned in consternation. *None of this is right. This is Horae Annaya, lady of Spring! She should be ruling in her palace, revered. I should be kneeling at her feet.*

It was a mercy that Kepi had been lucid—and kind, if the word could ever be used to describe her—to allow him to do this, as opposed to sending one of her other soldiers. *Or one of the shadow creatures,* Carulis shuddered. The other Horae hadn't been given such kindness, and he closed his eyes against the memories.

Many had suffered since Rama had been silenced.

1100 BC

Annaya woke to a dark morning. The deathly chill of winter stung the air, and she huddled in her blankets, wrapping the fleece tightly around her. Teeth chattering, she stumbled across the cold stone floor to the balcony, opening the shuttered doors to the dawn. It was the first day of spring. It should be. Yet the sun had not risen warm, the snows were not melting, and the birds were not returning.

A pale yellow glow from beyond the distant mountains lit the city below her. The sun was not in its strength, as it should be when Rama awoke and brought with her the life of spring.

What's gone wrong? Spring had never failed to arrive on the precipice of the vernal equinox before. Every generation of her family, spanning back as far as the history scrolls told, had been by

Rama's side as the representative Lady of Spring on this day—her mother, her mother's mother, and beyond.

Annaya walked the marbled halls of her mansion as the sun rose, her silk robes brushing the floor with every step. Slaves bustled about; cleaning and hanging the banners welcoming spring, preparing for the afternoon's feast celebrating the bounty to come. But today it rang hollow. She could see the lines of worry and fear the slaves shared with each other when they thought she wasn't looking.

What am I to do? Annaya was just as worried, but she couldn't let them see it. As Lady of Spring, she was the right hand of Rama—so why did she know nothing of this? Why could she not reach the catacombs and speak to the horned one?

The summons from Kepi came before her questions could be answered.

"My lady." One of her servant boys bowed as she opened her bedroom door to his knock. "There is a messenger at the door for you."

Whyever for? Annaya cocked her head. "Invite him in, offer him our hospitality. I will meet him in the viewing room after breakfast." The time for questions would be afterwards; no one could say they had entered her palace without being offered her full hospitality. *Gives me time to get dressed, too,* she thought wryly as she shut the door and headed over to her makeup table, shedding her night silks on the way.

Servant girls bustled around her, picking up her dresses; one unbinding her hair so it almost brushed the floor, before beginning braiding it again. Another patted blush onto her cheeks, and a fourth arranged her day's outfit.

The messenger, garbed in a red robe, draped in beads and chains, stood waiting in the viewing room as Annaya swished inside, his eyes downcast. He thanked her for her hospitality, before bowing and handing her the message roll.

Sealed with Queen Kepi's seal, Annaya noted, her heart skipping a beat. A message from the Queen herself. *This is bound to be good* . . . The Queen was, as her namesake, a tempest at the best of times. Completely unpredictable.

Annaya broke the red wax seal and unrolled the scroll with shaking fingers.

Queen and Our Lady Kepi, Ruler of the great and unconquerable Mycenaean Empire, requests the presence of the Lords and Lady of the Seasons, Horae of time past.

Queen Kepi will usher in a new era of Mycenaean rule, on this, a day on the precipice of the vernal equinox, and requires the Horae witnesses.

Winter chill gripped the land with icy fingers. On the day that the snows would melt, instead the land remained frozen, blanketed in white. Leaves did not burst forth from the trees, and the creatures of the land and sky remained in hiding.

Kepi, garbed in a robe of red and draped in golden chains, stepped up the white marble dais and spoke to the crowd gathered below. "Together, we will determine the course of our Empire and the world for years to come. Every year, we have gathered on these steps to carry out the transfer of power from the Lady of Winter, to the Lady of Spring. But that is the past. And now we are looking only to the future.

"We are assembled here today to issue a new decree to be heard in every city, in every foreign capital, and in every hall of power. From this day forward, a new vision will govern our land. *Gone* are the Horae, *gone* are the Lords and Ladies of the Seasons."

She gestured behind her, and a gasp rippled through the crowd. Silence fell, and not one word was spoken or breath taken in the entire cathedral as Mahomet rose to her feet.

She was a great, hulking beast; a massive black goat standing on her hind-legs. Bulging muscles rippled beneath her obsidian fur, and her hoofs, each bigger than a man's head, thudded on the marble floor. Mahomet tilted her head, bone-white horns thrusting from her skull and curving, twirling, to each side. Silver chains hung from her horns, clattering against each other as her glowing red eyes glared at the crowd.

Mahomet threw back her head, a shrill scream tearing out of her throat. A buzzing, swarming black cloud followed; a miasma pouring out of the goat god's jaws.

The blight entered the land.

1101 BC

True knowledge contains both good and bad, of life and death. Rama knew only the good: the life of spring. Mahomet balances the scales;

she knows death and blight, and only then do our people hold true knowledge.

Mahomet brought knowledge to the people of Mycenaea, and the downfall of the Horae. Queen Kepi celebrated the darkness of the long winter nights and short, cloudy days; the bone-chilling breeze that lingered in the air, the trees turned to mere skeletons, bare of leaves. The ground was black, hard-packed dirt on the paths, and a slurry of mud and snow in the alleyways. Children begged on the street corners, an all-too common sight. No farmer could afford to buy food, no food would grow for them to sell, and the world grew poorer. The plague ravaged the land.

Without the turning of the seasons, the Horae were slowly dying. Annaya, too, felt the scourge in her bones.

Annaya turned her head from the morose view. She'd long ago ceased to stop in the street to help the starving souls that cried out to her. They still recognised her as the Lady of Spring, despite Queen Kepi's constant attempts to disintegrate the bond of the Horae.

I believe Rama is still alive, fighting to break free from Mahomet's possession. We believe in Rama. Annaya thought.

A dilapidated house crouched at the end of the street; run-down, faded paint peeled from the walls, looking much like every other building in the city. The windows were dark, but Annaya didn't hesitate or knock, instead pushing the front door open.

Three men sat before a pale, flickering fire. It barely warmed the room; echoingly empty, with only a few scant furnishings, a painting hanging haphazardly on the wall showing a time when the grass grew and farmers tilled the fields.

Skorpios looked up from the fire, red coals reflecting in grey eyes, lined with wrinkles. "Kepi has called for the death of the Horae," he rasped.

Those words would have terrified her two years ago. Now, Annaya was neither surprised, nor could she really bring herself to feel anything. The mad Queen would do what the mad Queen would do.

"Where is there left to hide?" Annaya murmured, staring into the flames. The streets lay empty, footsteps echoing for what seemed like miles, if anyone dared walk them—or was left alive to do so. Not only were more than half the houses now abandoned, the remainder had survivors huddled inside, trying to survive against the plague. Everyone waited, hoping for an end to the hell that clung to every surface of the city.

Leander, Lord of Summer, sighed from his seat on the floor in the corner. "She keeps holding balls and feasts, though." The disdain in his voice was clear. "Celebrating this *true knowledge.* She doesn't know anything. She's been spared the pain of the plague, the pain of seeing family and friends die, of seeing a city bustling with life turn to a dark and abandoned place. She lives up in her white palace, full of her slaves and stores of food, while the rest of us starve and die."

Annaya leant back, crossing her arms over her chest. *How are we going to survive this?* There was hardly a world left to survive for. The other lands were too far to reach by any method other than caravan, and Queen Kepi had locked the roads down—and even then, the winter seemed to hold every town, every country in its grip. Not even traders and merchants could get in or out; she barely allowed enough trade to keep citizens alive, trapped in an eternal winter; the fields dry and dead, the beasts no longer giving milk.

Yet that ever-persistent will to live reared its head. There was no way out she could see, but by Rama, she was going to make one!

By Rama, indeed. That's who we really need right now. Annaya wracked her brain for possible solutions, as Leander and Skorpios— her other partner, Lord of Autumn--considered storming the palace. *With whom? We're three alone, without power. We'll be dead before we cross the first wall, let alone get through the third to the palace doors.*

"I—"

A knock at the door interrupted her. Leander raised his eyebrows, Skorpios jumped to his feet, alert. *No one just drops by for a friendly visit here . . .* Annaya tip-toed over to the door. She peered through the peephole before letting out a relieved sigh and swinging it open.

"Carulis!" She smiled, extending her hand. "It's been a very long time."

"It has." Her childhood friend's grip was strong, his hands rough. She'd seen him working at the smith before the blight, exchanged friendly words, but ever since the blight had fallen, no one had time for anyone else. Keeping themselves alive came first.

"Come, sit." She motioned to the fireplace and Leander slid off his stool beside the hearth, freeing up one of the few pieces of furniture in the room. "How on earth did you know to find me here?"

And why have you sought me out? Annaya thought. Of all people, what brings you to visit me?

Carulis perched on the edge of the rickety stool and rubbed his hands together in the scant warmth from the fireplace. He ran a few fingers through his hair; agitated, almost. "There's been word of Kepi's newest decree," he said softly, blue eyes staring up at her in concern. "Surely you've heard."

Annaya nodded.

"I thought as much. I knew I had to come to you as soon as I heard, in case you had not, and either way, to offer my services to help you. All of you." He motioned to the room. "We've all had enough of Kepi's madness. I served as a smith and as a soldier at her side after the blight. Not of my will," he added quickly, "but many were pressed into service when she came to fear for her life from her own citizens."

"And for good reason," Leander muttered, scowling as Annaya shot him a warning look. Such words were treason and they were all thinking it . . . but someone could be listening. *Then again, what is left to lose?*

"What're you offering us?" She asked, leaning forward.

"Hope."

What followed was hours of discussion—and arguments, if Annaya was honest with herself. Carulis offered plans and the two lords shot them down, offering their own for Carulis to point out the flaws. It felt like they were going in circles, left with nowhere to turn, when Carulis said something that stopped everyone in their tracks.

"What if *I* do it," he said slowly. "Kill the Horae. What if I accept Kepi's mission to rid her of the one last threat to her—and Mahomet's—rule?"

"Then *we'd* be dead," Leander hissed, "which defeats the point, doesn't it?"

Skorpios snorted, but Annaya held up a hand. "Wait, please. Carulis. What are you talking about?"

He stood in the snow, and she begged him to kill her.

Kepi chuckled at the vision wavering before her, a glowing tapestry hovering in the air between Mahomet's claws.

"Do *it*," she hissed, eyes alight with glee.

Carulis raised his dagger, then brought it down in one swift movement. Annaya toppled over, a pool of red staining the white snow beneath her.

Mahomet shut her claws with a snap. "The last is gone," she rumbled, ochre eyes glowing in the darkness of the Queen's chamber. "There remains no threat to bring us down. Rama will sleep forevermore, and you, my Queen, will rule over an eternal winter."

Kepi giggled. She spun round on her stool, suddenly serious, and began brushing her hair. "I will have a feast in celebration." She spoke to the demon's reflection. "A feast . . ." she said dreamily, running the brush through her long tresses.

Mahomet turned and left, but not without a disparaging glance at the mad Queen. A feast in the dead of the longest winter, when no one had food. When the palace kitchens were already scraping the bottom of the larder.

It was no concern of hers; if the Horae were dead and Rama slept forever, she would rule this place for centuries, millennia to come. All could die, for all she cared. The thought of ruling a world of death gave the beast a rush of exhilaration. Once Mycenaea was desolate, she would turn her gaze to the rest of Greece, consuming souls and spreading winter's death.

Annaya stood in the darkness, Carulis by her side. Leander and Skorpios shifted from foot to foot behind her, boots crunching in the snow as they waited for the sun to rise. It'd been simple enough to obtain a sack of pig's blood—no one watched the abandoned farms and the starving animals, instead hiding inside, waiting for death to take them. The creature had only had its suffering ended swiftly; it had been luckier than its fellows.

Carulis had said that Mahomet would be watching, with Kepi by the demon's side. If they made it look as though she'd been killed, the Queen's guard would be lowered for a moment.

"Until she realises you've disappeared, too." Annaya had pointed out earlier that morning as they waited in the snow.

Carulis sighed and shook his head. I have to go back. I can still help you, and help those still serving her in the palace from being taken from their beds and imprisoned for her amusement, and Mahomet's feeding."

Oh. Annaya fell silent. She didn't truly know the scope of the horrors Carulis had had to endure, to see and be unable to do anything; to even commit with his own hand. She shuddered. They all did what they had to in order to survive.

And this morning, at sunrise, they would call, using their combined powers as heralders of the seasons, and let their blood into the snow—their true blood this time—and summon Rama.

I hope this works. I hope she lives, and hears us. It has to . . . it's our only hope.

The pale yellow sun began its ascent from behind the mountains, and so ended their vigil as the summoning began.

Perhaps Rama would hear their cries and awaken, and their world could live once more. They had to try.

About the Author:

Jenna has been writing ever since she can remember! Born in Cairns, Queensland, in a family with a love for fantasy and sci fi novels, she didn't stand much of a chance. Paired with her love for animals—resulting in a short stint as a vet nurse, before running her own petsitting business—Jenna has been constantly writing, and has several science fiction & fantasy novels published on Amazon, with more to come!

THOSE ELECTRIC SHEEP NEED ELECTRIC GRASS

Brianna Bullen

The Shepherdess met us on the V/Line, the merchandise hidden under her golden fleece coat. She sat in the quiet carriage, headphones in, eyes down. Looked like any other disaffected twenty-something going through a quarter-life crisis; hair dyed straw-yellow under her hood, nails bitten down to the size of a small computer chip, and of course her hood with the sheep ears and curly ram horns that conformed to the quirky millennial standard. She was playing Pokemon on her phone, not even glancing up for her contact. The air gave my skin goosebumps, the heating on the train not enough to insulate against the reality of night. The Shepherdess' reflection was imposed over the inky blackness on the other side of the glass, overlaid in muted colours which were occasionally cut into by the lights and neon glow of the cities the train dashed passed. The effort of first contact was up to us, and while my partner and I were weird theatre kids, we were not good actors in the slightest. I hesitated, so Mary took the initiative.

"Shep! It's so good to see you after all this time!"

Shep did not look up from her phone. Mary waved a hand in front of her eyes and took out an earbud—a declaration of war if ever I'd seen one—and seemed surprised that all she got in return for her effort was a half-asleep glare as Shep buried deeper into her seat to avoid her. Shep put her headphone back in with the flick of her hair.

"Shep." Mary tried again. "Don't be like that. You know me. We met at Ino's party?"

The name of our contractor caused a reaction if you were paying attention on the micro-level. A slight widening of the eyes, before she returned to her bland expression. Her eyes darted to the yawning ticket inspector, who woke up an older man stinking of gin. "This is the quiet carriage," she said. "Please do not annoy me. Respect the social contract."

"Oh, please. There's hardly anyone in this carriage, we can afford to chat a bit. Catch up." Mary sat down next to her. Taking this as my cue, I sat down in the space across.

"Had Ino let me know you were such talkers, I would never have let her organise this meeting." Her lazy eyes glanced up from her phone, taking Mary in from Converse sneakers to snapback and finding her lacking. "I'd say take a seat, but you've already made yourselves at home. You guys had a wild night out? Your bra's showing, by the way. Might want to adjust the strap."

Shep reached into her jacket pocket as Mary grumbled about the perils of style and fixed her tank-top's coverage. Seeing the motion,

Mary quit grumbling and leant forward to smoothly take whatever Shep was offering—either the names of people willing to help us, or the bio-creature she'd managed to steal from the lab.

There was excitement: like a kid with sea-monkeys, just add it to water, and it'd grow. We couldn't wait to put it in the ocean. Let it clean up the waste, eat through the nets, heal the creatures. Take the wind out of the creators' sails by stealing it and letting it free before their allotted 'saving the day, hero style' hour. They could have saved life and the world earlier. They just let the catastrophe go on for optimal drama and fear, rather than intervening at the start when they had the technology. It kept them in business, after all. Gathered them more resources as people threw money at the government contractors to find a solution. They thought with their wallets, not their hearts. If they fixed it earlier, preventing such great loss, they wouldn't have made as much for themselves. Their company data showed they had created the fix prior to the event. They'd been holding onto it the entire time.

But instead, Shep whipped out her train ticket between her middle and forefinger with a sly smile, holding it out lazily for the inspector to validate with his machine. Didn't even spare a glance at the overworked man.

Mary and I both scrambled for our cards, Mary with a mumbled "thank you" and myself panicking, trying to remember if I had tapped on and that we weren't going to be interrupted further for fare evasion. I let out a relieved sigh as soon as the machine let out its happy ticking sound.

Shep smirked, but it was almost a bored smirk, half-checked out of the conversation. "You're a twitcher, aren't you? Don't be so keyed up. Don't look like the human equivalent of Instagram poetry. We're just having a conversation."

Telling someone to be less anxious is an incantation to make them even more anxious. I tittered like an owl stepping on a precariously weak branch. Just a conversation? This moment could change the world. All worlds. It got Mary to laugh though.

Shep's smirk just grew, before dropping to a scowl at motion from the other end of the carriage. A few men—conspicuously dressed in business suits and sunglasses, despite the midnight hour—had shuffled their way into the carriage, eyes no doubt glancing for anyone suspicious. I tried not to breathe too heavily. Prayed we had not been ratted out.

Shep let out an obnoxiously loud laugh, reached for my wrist. "Man, it's been years since I've seen someone with a watch who wasn't over fifty. You're a strange one. Why don't you just use your phone, or an internal accurate timer? The brain surgery's pain-free and harmless, I swear. I have the number of a good surgeon, let me get it for you." she reached into her pocket and continued to make a fuss about my watch. Pulled out a piece of paper that, from a distance, looked like a business card. Up close it was smoky glass with the micro-organism inside. I tried not to gasp as I took it, re-evaluating what kind of person our contact was. Adrenaline junky, to risk a trade under the noses of men clearly packing guns. There was a brightness to her eyes which hadn't been there before.

The audacity. Her gaze flashed to the men, all of whom seem to deem us as just three women out partying.

They left the carriage, moving onto the next. One of them tipped their head in a nod as he passed, as if saying 'have a pleasant evening'.

Shep smirked, went back to looking at her nails. "Too easy. Fucking idiots."

"I wonder who tipped them off," I murmured, mentally reeling through lists of contacts and names within the organisation.

"I have my suspicions." Shep fiddled with the felt ram horn on her hoodie before texting. I could see Ino's name on her screen. "Only gave one person the time, they've been under suspicion for a bit. Ino will deal with them."

"And they don't know your face?"

"Nup. To them, I'm just the ram."

I'd seen the footage. The skeletal ram's face morphed over her own as a mask. The violent charges. Taking down men twice her size, liberating chicken farms and pinching important documents. Unrefined, until Ino got the footage and found the girl. As soon as that mask was on, she was more beast than human. More avenger than saviour. Looking at the woman in front of me, her tight smile, I could believe it.

Her eyes darted like a fox to the train's doors, making sure the men had gone. "So what do you think of the number? Going to give it a call?"

I looked at the tiny creature, embryonic, seemingly covered in stars. Light glowed out of its pores. "If you think it'll have a positive impact?"

"Trust me," she grinned. "I know it will."

The day the eco-fighters turned the tides was the day I fell in love.

About the Author:

Brianna Bullen is a Deakin University PhD creative writing candidate writing about memory in science fiction. She has had work published in journals including LiNQ, Aurealis, Voiceworks, Rabbit, Multiverse: An anthology of international science fiction poetry, and Woolf Pack Zine.

She won the 2017 Apollo Bay short story competition and placed second in the 2017 Newcastle Short story competition. Her manuscript was previously a finalist in the 2018 Subbed In Poetry Chapbook competition. In 2018, she was part of Nexus, an Arts Access Victoria collective for artists with mental health recovery lived experience.

FOUR HOURS OF INSTABILITY

Aiki Flinthart

"What the *fuck* do you mean, 'it's not there'?" I leaned over, deliberately using my bulk to intimidate. It was a useful tactic. I was a big guy. It saved a lot of boring arguments. Arguments I had no time for right now.

This woman just raised her chin and glared at me. "I mean," she said in the slow, deliberate tones of someone speaking to an idiot, "that particular line is gone. Successfully folded in. Done. No longer an option for hopping. Anything about that not make sense . . ." she flicked a look at the pips on my shoulder that denoted five hundred hops, fifty-two folds and fifty-eight saves. ". . . *Major* Joshua Singh?"

I tugged the jacket of my severe black uniform down. She was right, of course, I just didn't want to hear it. The chronoliser on my wrist bleeped softly and flashed a yellow warning light. I swore again and sank onto a damnably-hard grey bench nearby.

Snatching off my black cap, I ran a hand over the soft bristles of my crewcut black hair and the harder bristles on my chin. I must look like crap. Six months of back-to-back hops and the shadows under my eyes were almost darker than my irises.

But we were so damned close now.

We were all working towards the same end: the hoppers, the line controllers, and the syncers. We all wanted the same thing: a single, unfractured, peaceful timeline. Then to live linear for a while. At least until some other arrogant moron came along and screwed it up again.

So, who'd authorised this fold of my line? And how had they fucked it up so thoroughly?

"This is bad," I muttered, checking my chronoliser. Four hours.

The woman's eyes widened. She glanced back at the holo display, the hub of the control room—a spider's tangle of thin, glowing lines that grew and divided like tree branches from a thick central core. Their glowing tips inched ever upward and outward, second by second, microscopically. When I'd started work here, it had been a giant ball, with more lines than any human could count. Now the end was in sight—but maybe not for me.

She crouched before me, violet eyes searching my face. She flicked back a ponytail of straight chestnut hair. Only then did I see the pips on her jacket. Seven hundred hops, sixty-six folds, and sixty-nine saves. I straightened.

"Sorry, Major . . ." I read her nametag: *Amanda Greenway* ". . . Greenway. Didn't see your rankings. Spoke out of turn. It's just that . . ." I swallowed, my gaze drifting back to the mesmerising holo display. One of the branches darkened and faded, vanishing to nothing, right back to its lowest branch. I groaned.

"Was it your line? The one you asked me about?" She sat beside me. Around us the ops room continued in its hushed busyness. Grey sound-absorbent floors and walls. Silver, grey and black chrondatabanks, operated by syncers, like Greenway, in their dark grey uniforms. Line controllers spoke to hoppers through the subvocal coms embedded into the skin of their throats—a dozen or more intense youngsters standing around the massive holo image, checking, scanning, referring back to the submolecular notes in their glove linesyncs. Always alert for fuckups.

So, how had they missed this one?

Greenway was still waiting for an answer.

I nodded. "89beta was mine. A shitty, wardump of a line, but 89 is still my birthline and beta's the only one I survived to recruitment age in. Is it really folded?"

She frowned and stared at the miniature holo image hovering above her linesync glove. It responded to the thought patterns converted by the nanotech in her temple and fed information back to her. I shuddered. Why had she given up hopping to take a sync job? Syncers and line controllers were bonded so tightly to the holo they stayed until death. And they usually started as teenagers and died young. What gave someone that kind of martyr complex? Greenway was by far the oldest in the group. Closer to my linear age of forty.

"Definitely folded, Singh," she said briskly. "No mistake. Looks like we found the crucial kill just before the Secondary Event. Once he was dead, that folded 89beta back in to 89alpha perfectly, along with 89gamma right through to sigma so far. The effects are still cascading. It'll take a few hours to be sure of the extent. Neat job, actually. Alpha's primed to fold into mainline, now. Captain Weller gets the fold credit. Still, they should have made sure . . ."

The images flashed across her holo too fast for me to interpret. Subliminal visions of people's faces, facts, data, names, consequences.

Then the holo vanished and her face blanked. She rose. "Sorry, Major. Nothing to be done. I suggest you keep that well-charged until they can reinstate you." She nodded to the chronoliser on my wrist.

I stood. "What the fuck was that about, Greenway? Weller folded my line without saving me? What did you see? Why was it folded without notice? No one warned me. No one stabilised me." I thrust my arm out and the chronoliser blinked orangish. "And now all you can say is keep this charged?" I grabbed her wrist. "Without this, I'm gone. You know that. Like I never existed."

She stared coldly back. "Take your hand off me, Major. I outrank you by fourteen folds and eleven saves. I'll have no hesitation in reporting you." Her mouth twisted. "But if you don't go charge your chronoliser now, that won't be necessary, will it?"

She jerked her chin at the door. "Now, go. I'll come check on you when my shift's done. Half an hour." Her violet eyes held some sort of message my hop-thickened brain was too sluggish to interpret. Numb, I spun away and left the room.

I stalked blindly through grey, low-lit corridors, following the subtle tug of my chronoliser towards my allocated room. Coming back from a hop, one never knew what had changed. A room allocation, wall colour, the name of the station cat. Never anything important. Minor things that were easy to assimilate or ignore. Just part of hopper life. A small price to pay for folding it all back into the single, peaceful line.

Minor, until now. Being eliminated from history was a pretty fucking big change.

I reached my room and the door slid open to my chronosignature. At least it still recognised me. Something, anyway. The room contained nothing but a slab bed, two chairs, a small table and a holo of my parents. There was no point in collecting possessions that might vanish after the next fold.

I slugged back a shot of restorative fifty-eight. Tasted like a cross between pure alcohol and cut grass. Revolting, but it woke me up and I sank onto a chair, staring blankly at the holo of my parents. Their sombre brown faces still stared back at me. Which meant their lives at the point that image was taken weren't affected by the folding. Hardly surprising. The holo still had been captured six years before Event One divided the world into a hundred plus wartorn lines, and sixteen years before the secondary Event that fractured 89alpha into ten sub-lines.

I'd been born just a few days before Event One. In early April. I shook my head. Like that mattered. My father always said it made me stubborn and determined. I figured the shit that had happened to us had more to do with it. My doctor-mother and younger sister had been killed when I was four. My engineer father was crippled in the same bomb blast. I'd grown up a street-rat, living hand-to-mouth, a thief at five, a killer at nine, recruited by the hoppers at seventeen.

I'd spent the last twenty-three linear years gladly hunting down Event radixes. Eliminating them in the hopes of eliminating the wars that killed my mother and sister.

That was the goal, after all. Undo all the minor fractures, one by one, until we were able to finally narrow down the one Event that had begun the whole damned mess.

Then we could fold back into the only line that had a peaceful outcome. The one line Admin had decided was the best result for mankind.

Mainline.

I laughed bitterly. Most of mankind. Not me, apparently.

Now, someone had found the secondary Event for my line and undone it—folded my line back into 89alpha.

I'd seen what folding did; what happened to families, towns, governments, whole countries, sometimes—gone. I knew it was for the greater good. But I'd never expected it to happen to me.

My head ached just trying to imagine how my death might have happened. I'd been in a lot of pretty damned dire situations in the years between 89's secondary Event and being recruited by Chrono Admin. Any one of which could have ended me. Had ended me.

Dammit.

My chronoliser blinked reddish. Three and a half hours left. Greenway was right. I should charge it. I only existed because it kept a record of me; constantly refreshing the central databank and reminding this limbo-world-between-lines "reality" of my existence.

There were supposed to be safeguards against this shit happening. They told us when we were recruited: no matter what happens, you're guaranteed a life in the Mainline. Every time we stop an Event, they said, we ensure any hoppers in that line will still exist. You work for us and we promise you'll live a full life in the Mainline.

They held out the promise of peace and plenty to those, like me, tempered, trained, and embittered by a childhood of fear and death. A lure too great to resist. Even if it meant a life away from loved ones.

I tore off the badge denoting fifty-two saves and threw it across the room. Fifty-two other hoppers would live because of me. Because I'd taken the time to ensure their survival even as their Event ceased to happen and their line folded back in. But some asshole hadn't bothered to check my lifeline when he folded 89beta.

The door light flashed.

"Fuck off," I muttered.

"It's Greenway."

"Shit. Fine. Open." I dialled another two restoratives, this time with double alcohol, and set them on the small metal table.

The door slid open and Greenway slipped in. She thumbed the lock code on the door and peered down the corridor outside, just before the door shut.

I rose, frowning.

"What the fu—"

Her warm lips on mine shut me up effectively. I froze for an instant, then relaxed into the kiss. Unexpected, but not unpleasant. She melted into my arms and pressed her lean body against me, deepening the kiss with an urgency that spoke of desperation, until I had to break free and hold her off to catch my breath and slow things down a little.

I frowned down at her and she gazed back, panting. Then her eyes widened and she stepped away.

"Shit." She leaned heavily on the wall and pressed her lips together. "You don't remember me, do you, Josh?"

I twisted a half-smile. "You'd be pretty damned hard to forget, so no, I don't. Should I? As far as I'm aware, we met today in the control room."

She paced twice across the small room, two fingers pressed to her forehead. "It's starting sooner than I expected."

"What?"

"It's Captain Weller," she said, her movements abrupt, impatient. "He's the one doing this."

"Look, Greenway . . . Amanda." I changed the name at her stricken look. "Robert Weller is one of the best hoppers we have. What is it you think he's doing?"

She paced a couple more times then collapsed into the other chair as though her reserves had drained. She downed the restorative and made a face. "That's foul. Now I know for sure you don't remember me. I hate that one."

I sat opposite and gripped her restive hands. "Tell me. Are we talking memory purge? Do you think Weller's purged my mind? I thought that was a myth."

"I thought so, too, but it's the only explanation for you forgetting me." She nodded. "And for why Weller was sent to your line to do the fold. He must have found out. *They* must have found us out."

"Found what out? Start back a little further. Assume I don't know what the fuck you're talking about, because you'd be right."

Amanda gave a weak chuckle. "You and I, and about six other hoppers. For six months now we've been working against the Chrono Admin. Trying to stop them from folding us all into one line."

"Why the hell would we do that?" I'd seen the Mainline. Even stayed there on holidays a few times. Not a goddamned bomber in sight. No hunger, no poverty, no blood spattering the walls like sick gothic modern artwork. Idyllic.

"Some of us don't want our lines to be folded," she said quietly. "They weren't so bad. Not as bad as the Chrono makes out, at least. Not perfect, of course."

"Then you were lucky," I said harshly. "Because mine was a hellhole of the worst kind. There is no fucking way I would be helping your little subversion. We need Mainline. We need peace. I want my family to live in that world, not one where a nine-year-old has to kill to survive."

I rose and strode to the door. "Now get out before I report you."

"You don't understand," she said, staying where she was though her face was pale. "You found out what was happening before you left on your last hop. You were determined to stop it. Blindly, utterly determined. You wouldn't listen to me when I said we couldn't." Her mouth twisted. "But you never listen to me, anyway."

"Stop what?" I hesitated. She wasn't wrong about my habit of cheerfully ignoring advice I didn't want to hear.

"Chrono isn't saving us any more."

"Who?" I said, "You or the whole of humanity?"

"Us. Hoppers." She pointed to me and herself. "At least, not all of us. Just a chosen few. That was why I quit hopping. So I could see for myself after two of my friends just . . . disappeared. I found out Chrono isn't keeping us like they promised. They're letting us die off, one by one. Captain Weller's leading the team that's doing it. They're just preventing Events and letting hoppers from certain lines die. And they always die. Somehow. Even the ones living peaceful lives in their folded lines."

I frowned. "Why the hell would Weller do that? Doesn't it cause loop paradoxes up and down the lines?"

She shook her head. "We were told it would, when we were recruited. Told that if you kill the hoppers who've folded various lines, then the lines unfold again. That sort of thing. But it's not true. I don't know how they're doing it, but the lines are staying folded. Which means—"

"They're getting close to Event One," I breathed. "That's the only explanation."

"But why kills us off? It makes no sense," she said. "After all we've done. Why would they renege?"

"Because," I said slowly, drawing a long breath, "we're a loose end." I whirled and stared intently at her. "If they fold everything back into the Mainline, then what's the worst threat to everlasting peace?"

She frowned, then her face cleared and her jaw dropped. "Another cataclysmic Event. And the only thing that could create one would be a hopper with intimate knowledge of all the key world events up and down the Mainline. And the installed nanotech to hop back and cause the Event. But who would do that? Why?"

I snorted. "Have you been to Mainline?"

"Sure. Holidays. Training runs. The usual." Her soft lips quirked into a half-smile. "I was born two hundred linears ago, so I've visited a few descendants to make sure they turn out alright."

"We all do that," I said absently. "But there's one thing we never really notice—because Admin don't let us stay long in the Mainline."

"Which is?"

I stretched my lips into a savage smile. "How fucking boring it is. Everyone's *nice*. Everyone obeys rules. Everyone's conscientious and hardworking and so fucking happy it makes your teeth ache after a few months. We hoppers don't quite . . . fit in. Most of us carry too many years of death in our heads. We don't think the same as the natives."

Her violet eyes widened. "How do you know what it's like after a few months?"

I threw back another restorative and coughed. "Because I've been with Weller on a deep cover Event One recon. We stayed a year. Almost drove me insane. Who else has been folded without being saved?"

She paused, thought, then said, "Wu, Otaga, Hassan, M'temba and Blake."

"Wu as well? Dammit." An aching hole opened in my chest and pain fisted around my larynx. I stared at my hands, brooding. Wu and I had been lovers for that year. The excitement of sneaking around and hiding our relationship a temporary relief from the mind-numbing dullness of conformity.

I cleared my throat. "That's the whole team who went to Mainline with Weller and I for that year. I'm the last, then. Barring Weller, himself." My knees gave way and I sat hard on the unforgiving seat. "I thought we'd failed."

Amanda cocked her head. "At what?"

"Finding the crucial kill to stop Event One. But Weller must have found it and not told us. And he's killing us off, just in case anyone *does* work out the cause and tries to prevent the kill." I frowned. "Or maybe tries to steal whatever tech caused Event One in the first place. We never worked that out, either."

Amanda dropped to her knees on the soft grey floor before me and grabbed my wrists. "Maybe you know it, too! Or Weller thinks you know. Maybe you have the information in your head, somewhere. That's why they've started the memory purge. We must get you to a mindmapping station. Quickly. Once we know for sure, we can restore your line as well."

She rose, hauling on my arm.

"Restore line 89beta?" I rose, frowning. "Seriously?"

She nodded vigorously. "Like I said. Some of us don't want to Mainline. We want our homes. Once we know who Weller's kill target is to prevent Event One, we can stop him. Then we can undo the fold on your line, at least. It's only fair. But we need to get to the mindmapper."

"Do you know how to work one?" I asked. "I'd rather not be wiped if you get it wrong."

She hesitated, biting her lip and eyeing me uncertainly. I moved in closer and slid my arms around her waist.

"I might have been memory-purged of some things, but I'm damned sure I want to remember you this time," I murmured. Now it was my turn to kiss her and I took the time to enjoy it. Her lips softened and parted. I pulled her close, running a hand down her back to her arse. With the other I dragged the tie from her hair and slid my fingertips across her scalp. I deepened the kiss, tongues tangling, lips warm and sensual. She groaned and her fingernails scraped down my back.

We broke apart, panting. She glanced at the bed and flushed. I smiled faintly.

"If we're going to check what's in my brain and stop Weller," I murmured, stroking her throat with a fingertip, "we'll have to do it soon." I held up my wrist and showed her the flashing red light. "Three hours."

Her eyes opened wide and she pulled back. "Why didn't you charge it? A mindmap can take hours."

I shrugged. "I was about to when you turned up." I grinned wickedly. "We could find a way to pass half an hour while it charges, I'm sure."

She shook her head and retied her ponytail with quick, sharp movements. "No time. We'll rig a charger next to the mindmapper. Let's go."

"Wait," I said. "If I'm going to help you, I want to know who the others are you're working with. And I want assurance I'll have somewhere to live that can keep charging my chronoliser once we leave here. In case you can't restore 89beta. Not all of the lines have this sort of tech."

Amanda wiped her palms down her thighs and eyed me narrowly. "Fine. Yokota, Helms, Fingaardson, and Espana. Wu and Blake were with us, too." She gripped my hand and looked deep into my eyes. "We'll restore 89beta, I promise. We'll find a way to be together."

"Thankyou." I straightened and flicked my cap back onto my head. "Weller? Did you get all that?"

My door slid open and Robert Weller entered, flanked by four burly guards carrying stun weapons.

Greenway gaped and backed away. She cast me a pleading look. "What are you doing, Josh? We're not your enemy, he is. He's the one who killed you. He's the one who killed all your team, remember? Purged your memory of us. We just want to live in our own lines. What's wrong with that? Help us!"

I shook my head. "Too late. I've seen the other lines. Yours might have been alright two hundred linears ago, when you were born, but now every fucking one is a hellhole of human misery."

Cocking my head, I shrugged. "And there's no such thing as a memory purge. We never met until today. You just wanted to get me into the mindmapper so you could find Event One. Nice try, though. Get her out, Weller."

The four guards manhandled her, protesting, from the room. I sighed and sank back onto the chair.

Robert sat in the chair Amanda had vacated and dialled up two drinks. He slid one to me and lifted his in salute. He downed it and coughed, his grey eyes tearing up.

He ran a hand through his short, blond hair and waited for me to speak. Letting people fill uncomfortable silences with stupid words was one of his strengths. Lean and intense, he was a linear decade younger than me, but so sharp several people had cut themselves on him.

I held up my wrist with the chronoliser and studied it pensively. "When I was nine, I broke into a house looking for something to steal. Instead I killed a man. It was an accident. He surprised me. I shot him."

"I know," Weller said, his deep voice quiet.

I sent him a shrewd look. "When?"

Weller shrugged. "The year we were undercover in Mainline. I did some research. Hopped over to 89alpha and beta on the sly.

Realised that you'd killed the one man who could prevent Event Three in that line. And in several other lines as well."

"How?" I asked, turning the full glass on the table, back and forth, until the scrape annoyed me and I threw the drink down my throat in one burning gulp.

He leaned back, threading his fingers across his stomach. "The man you killed now goes on, instead, to imprison the man responsible for the 89alpha Event Two—before it happens when you're ten. Event Two was caused by an engineer who created a temporal distortion weapon of unthinkable destructive power. He called it The Ram." He shrugged again. "But, in his defence, the engineer was actually trying to do something that he thought would be very simple."

"Which was?" I held the glass so tight my knuckles whitened.

Weller's lean hand pried the glass loose and gripped my fingers. His gaze was sympathetic.

"Prevent a bombing before it happened. To save a woman who died in that bombing."

I twisted a wry smile. "There were a lot of bombings in 89alpha. And a lot of women died."

Weller's lips turned up in an empty copy of my expression. "But that wasn't the engineer's first attempt. His previous was more successful. The woman had originally died—of childbirth complications—in the year of Event One. The engineer invented The Ram, went back, and caused Event One. The woman and her child survive the childbirth trauma in every line he created—"

"Except Mainline." I gave a bitter laugh and fiddled with the chronoliser on my wrist.

"Right. In Mainline the engineer kills himself when he finds out about her death, and the child's death. So, he never invents The Ram."

I closed my eyes, trying to remember the future. Then I stripped off the chronoliser with a sharp movement and held it out to him. "Do me a favour?"

He raised his brows. "Anything, Josh, you know that. We've been friends a long time. Anything in my power." The lines around his mouth deepened and his grey eyes were stormclouds in a stoic expression.

"When you kill the engineer before he marries my mother, make sure she lives a better life this time?"

I dropped the chronoliser into his open hand.

About the Author:

The Reborn Sun

Emilie Morscheck

Eliza rolled onto her right side, the mattress depressing underneath her with a groan. Her hand rested on the curvature of her expanded belly, nerves searching for any sign of life. There was a hollowness to her body and she fought away the anxious thought that there was something wrong with her baby.

She rolled again, hoping to prompt a kick. The child was still.

The clock read 5:30a.m. Eliza forced herself to get up, feet swinging onto the carpet. She stretched her legs walking to the bathroom, relieved her bladder.

She examined her belly, admiring the dark veins that curled under her skin, the bulge of her belly button.

Her baby would live.

Eliza woke, hands bloody and gravel pressed to her face. She was a few metres from the door of the car—the car which was twisted around a post—airbags inflated, glass shattered, her husband's body in the front seat. Limp. Smoke caught in the back of her throat. A coughing fit overcome her as she twisted down to see her stomach, punctured, bleeding. A cry left her throat as she stumbled to her knees.

A warm rush of red spilled down her thighs as the air filled with sirens. She returned to the ground, hot tears burning her face.

The old woman had told her of the field, with its wildflowers that swayed through the long grasses, the distant trees that enclosed it, and the ram that grazed in its centre. Eliza carried her husband's pocketknife in her left fist, blade flicked open. She approached the ram. In the pure sunlight, the wool looked almost golden, shimmering in the unusually hot spring day.

The ram lifted its head, black eyes watching Eliza as she approached. It did not move and the flowers in the meadow hung in the air as the breeze dropped.

Eliza continued with a steady pace until she was close enough to reach forward with her free hand and sink it into the soft wool. Undisturbed, the ram returned to the grass.

A cold tear caught in the corner of Eliza's eye. This is what the old woman had told her to do.

She pulled the knife across the ram's throat, the deep red gushed out, coating her fingers and splashing on her bare feet. The ram shook, back legs collapsing. Eliza released the convulsing body, waiting for the life to drain away.

Panting, she knelt by the carcass and began to skin the animal. It took her longer than she thought, and she recoiled at its intense heat. But the golden wool was hers.

Eliza wrapped her baby in a soft woollen blanket. She had golden eyes and a small curl of pale hair on her head. Together they sat in the garden even though the weather was too cold to do so. Baby Helen didn't cry. She was a silent little thing.

"Your daughter," she said, raising Helen to the engraved stone that bore her husband's name. "Isn't she *perfect?*"

About the Author:

Emilie Morscheck is the Australian author of speculative short stories and novels. While working on her first novel she found the time to study engineering and arts at the Australian National University. Emilie was a participant of the Toolkits Fiction program and a creative editor at the ANU's student paper Woroni. Her works on Wattpad.com have over 50,000 reads. In 2019 Emilie received an artsACT grant to edit her YA fantasy novel "The Girl with the Knife". She is a fan of kelpies, selkies and watery graves. @EmilieMorscheck

Non-Human Resources

A. G. Jones

Of all the tribulations Seamus Kent had navigated as Human Resources Manager at Thomas, Arthur and Jones Accounting, today had the potential to be his biggest challenge yet. It was certainly greater than the birthday cake gaffe of '03 when Sarah Glendale from reception turned out to be both a celiac and vegan; bigger than the mixed softball team of '07 that included no women; and was quite possibly of more significance than the water cooler incident of '09; although Seamus was confident that today was unlikely to involve half a dozen paramedics.

The gravitas of the situation had dawned on Seamus when Cecil Arthur, partner and namesake of Thomas, Arthur and Jones Accounting, delivered the news on Friday afternoon. Seamus was of the firm belief that Cecil Arthur did not like him for the simple reason that Seamus was terrible at golf. Cecil Arthur preferred to conduct business on the back nine, and with a handicap that suggested that Seamus would spend the better part of a day on the course looking for a golf ball, rather than hitting it, the infrequent meetings Seamus had with Cecil Arthur had not endeared the HR Manager to one of his three bosses. The fact that Cecil Arthur had spoken to Seamus without wearing a white, leather glove, and tartan pants, emphasised the significance of their brief discussion.

Seamus had spent the better part of the weekend scrutinizing the message's subtext with the ferocity that Harold Prince would give to the dramaturgy of one of his Tony Award winning musicals. After replaying the meeting in his head more times that his own nuptial vows, Seamus was certain that Mr Arthur's three sentences spoke volumes:

Kent (I am using your surname without an honorific to reinforce an appropriate hierarchy between employee and partner).

We have a green one starting on Monday (Not only is Thomas, Arthur and Jones Accounting a proud name in asset and investment management, we also invest our social capital into making a better world. You are needed, Kent, for this very task in welcoming our first non-human employee to the firm).

Make him feel welcome (with your fifteen years' experience in Human Resources, that included managing the aftermath of the water cooler incident of '09, I couldn't think of anyone better qualified to pioneer the expansion of the Human Resources Portfolio to include non-humans as well).

Don't fuck up! (Although the partners and I at Thomas, Arthur and Jones Accounting have absolute faith in you, I can't stress enough the importance of making a good first impression to our very first Orcish employee. You are the front-line of a firm that endeavours to welcome non-human employees into a historically human dominated industry. In its simplest form, Thomas Arthur and Jones Accounting wants you, Kent, to be our face for change).

Armed with the faith of Cecil Arthur of Thomas, Arthur and Jones Accounting no less, and an appreciation of the grandeur of the situation, Seamus Kent awaited the new Orcish employee from behind the desk in the Human Resources office. *Non-Human Resources now*, he chuckled to himself, and filed the witticism in his mental cabinet under 'zingers'. It was a file he regularly drew on around the water cooler to cut through the foreboding atmosphere that still lingered around the most accessible hydration point on the 24th floor.

The phone rang at 8:59 with a call from reception. "Your 9:00, Mr Nurghed Stonebutter, is here."

Punctual to an acceptable point, Seamus thought. Seamus Kent made Mr Stonebutter wait until 9:15 to let him in. It was move number twenty-three—'The powerful can afford to make you wait'—in Kenneth Brigg's self-help book, *55 Moves for Business Success.*

After the news of Brigg's incarceration, Seamus wondered if he should still follow the advice of a man whose arrest for insider trading suggested at least one move hadn't led to business success. He was inadvertently reassured by Terrance Jones of Thomas, Arthur and Jones Accounting, who was an obvious disciple of Briggs. In a stroke of genius, Terrance Jones had once used rule twenty-three and made Seamus wait three hours before admitting him into his office. He then expertly executed rule fourteen, 'Wasted time weakens the value of your time,' by only giving Seamus thirty seconds to explain the outcome of the most recent sexual harassment complaint filed against the namesake of the accounting firm.

Not wanting to draw attention to the tusks that protruded from Nurghed Stonebutter's mouth, or the green hue of his face that was normal of his species (and coincidently similar to the sickly pallor of no less than thirty employees during the water cooler incident of '09), Seamus cast his gaze towards the expertly tied Double Windsor knot of Stonebutter's red tie.

While shaking hands, Seamus said "Mr Stonebutter, welcome. Cecil Arthur himself has asked me to welcome you to Thomas, Arthur and Jones Accounting." Seamus would later reflect on the handshake with two main thoughts, the first being Kenneth Brigg's TEDTalk, 'Handshakes for Success, it's all in the wrist' did not have Orcish employees in mind. Secondly, Seamus couldn't imagine Nurghed Stonebutter ripping a man's arms out of their socket to bludgeon the very same armless man to death. His hands were far too soft and moisturised.

During the socially acceptable ten minutes of small talk appropriate to building rapport with a new employee, Seamus Kent used a list of topics that he was confident would not give offense to Stonebutter's Orcish sensibilities. It turns out that like Seamus, Nurghed Stonebutter was also enjoying the moderate spring weather; had a forty to fifty minute morning commute, and while he enjoyed coffee, he limited himself to two a day.

As Seamus took Stonebutter for a tour of the office, he became confident that he had laid the foundation for a workplace association to build upon. Nurghed Stonebutter was attentive during the tour and only interjected with pertinent inquiries such as the appropriate font size and type used for in house communication and if a jacket was still required for Casual Fridays. Seamus assured him that a jacket was not necessary; however they both agreed that wearing jeans would take the casual nature of Casual Fridays too far. After-all, they were not sitting at home without the expectation of visitors.

While Seamus and Nurghed (a man and orc who were quickly becoming congenial, workplace associates) were nearing the water cooler on the twenty-fourth floor, Seamus felt confident in taking a calculated risk. Seamus shared his *Non-Human Relations* zinger with Nurghed, who was a most receptive audience. His throaty chuckle let out a hint of Nurghed's restrained power.

The chortle was loud enough that David 'tightrope' Blondin—nicknamed for his ability to balance the most convoluted of accounts—looked up with irritation from his computer, but quickly retracted his head back into his cubicle when he realised that the individual he was about to chastise could most easily balance David over his head while still having a spare hand free to answer the telephone.

When the elevator opened on the twenty-fourth floor, it revealed the unfortunately named Thomas Thomas, the first listed partner of Thomas, Arthur and Jones accounting. Thomas Thomas was the third Thomas Thomas in the Thomas family and in true Thomas tradition, Thomas Thomas of Thomas, Arthur and Jones accounting had also named his eldest son Thomas Thomas.

When the youngest Thomas Thomas came home and complained of his inherited name, his father repeated the same words that Great-Grandfather Thomas Thomas and Grandfather Thomas Thomas had said to their respective sons. "Thomas is a fine name and suggestive of such a fine character, that one should be proud to have it twice."

And like every Thomas Thomas that had passed on their names, they hoped that the good-natured ribbing their sons would receive on account of their inheritance would help them live up to the Thomas Thomas name.

In an attempt to avoid such ribbings which had often resulted in either bruising, a mouthful of toilet water, or a combination of both, Thomas Thomas had developed a bookish attitude in his early years. While Seamus Kent would be hesitant to think poorly of any of the founders of Thomas, Arthur and Jones accounting, he had to use a thesaurus to find a better word than 'awkward' to describe Thomas Thomas. He has decided on 'maladroit' and was satisfied that should he ever be asked to describe Thomas Thomas, he could be both honest and confident that most of his coworkers wouldn't know what he meant.

"Good morning Mr Thomas," Seamus said. "Might I introduce the newest member of the firm, Mr Nurghed Stonebutter."

When Thomas Thomas noticed Nurghed Stonbutter towering above him, Seamus thought that his boss looked like one of the three little pigs, who upon leaving his home, hadn't noticed the strategically placed cooking pot that had replaced his door mat. Nor had he noticed the cartoonish wolf wearing a large, red napkin and holding a knife and fork. Seamus Kent saw Thomas Thomas' eyes bulge before the partner of Thomas, Arthur and Jones Accounting sprinted into the elevator.

Seamus wasn't surprised that Thomas Thomas hadn't opened the email informing the firm of their first non-human employee, and assumed that Thomas Thomas had not seen Stonebutter's impeccably tied Double Windsor, an uncharacteristic clothing choice for a creature Thomas Thomas must have assumed was here to murder and pillage his way across the twenty-fourth floor.

Stonebutter chuckled about the awkward interaction with his new employer, which Seamus Kent was most grateful for.

Not wanting to derail the otherwise seamless induction, Seamus took Nurghed Stonebutter to the staffroom for lunch. It was 11:45, slightly early for Seamus, but he knew that Marg Smith—the longest serving receptionist of the firm—would be having lunch. Marg's inability to use the possessive apostrophe and her insistent use of kitten pictures at the bottom of her office emails had led Seamus to vigorously squeeze his stress ball on more that on occasion; however, Seamus also knew that Marg Smith could make anyone feel welcome. Her open and welcoming disposition was the polar opposite of her husband, Cecil Smith, who managed dispatch. Seamus did not know why an accounting firm needed dispatch, but as it had been a part of the firm as long as Cecil Smith, management assumed that it must be important. Seamus tried to be friendly with Cecil Smith, however he did not look forward to informing Cecil Smith that the 'Green Face' costume he had worn to the Halloween Party the last 15 years, would no longer be acceptable.

Marg smiled warmly at Stonebutter's introduction, she had applied her husband's makeup every Halloween and must have become accustomed to orcish looking gentleman. Her own makeup this day gave little suggestion of her age. The trowel she used to apply her foundation created an even rendering that hid most of her facial crevices.

"I was just reading the horoscopes. Would you gents care to know what to expect today?" asked Marg.

"I'm not sure what my human star sign is, Mrs Smith."

"Please, it's Marg, and not to worry. When were you born, Mr Stonebutter?"

"Orcs don't tend to celebrate their birthdays, but for my identification, I believe my mother said it was early April."

Marg ran her finger down the newspaper, "Ah! That makes you an Aries then, Mr Stonebutter."

"Please Marg, Nurghed is fine."

"Okay then, Murfdhed, Aries the ram."

"I can hardly be a ram, Marg. My brothers would have eaten me already," said Nurghed before all three of them laughed.

Seamus was impressed by Nurghed's desire to make a good first impression. He glossed over Marg's poor pronunciation of his name without his charm wavering.

Seamus didn't give much stock to cosmology, a man who ironed his own socks would hardly put his faith in the stars to guide him. Nevertheless, Seamus listened on while Marg read to Nurghed in a soft, presumably sagely tone.

"When was the last time you stopped to kindle a new friendship, Aries? When did you last make a new friend? Not one that merely likes your posts, but one with a kindred spirit? Now is the time to be open to new relationships, to spend the extra time around the water cooler, the changerooms, or the supermarket aisle, for no other reason than to enjoy another's company."

If it had been 1:30pm, Seamus' scheduled time for his second coffee, he might have choked on it. New friendships, water cooler! Was there something to this horoscope business? Nurghed smiled and looked at Seamus. The Human Resources Manager at Thomas, Arthur and Jones Accounting wondered if their first non-human employee was thinking the same thing.

Seamus and Nurghed fetched their lunches from the staff fridge. As always, Seamus had two tuna and mayonnaise sandwiches wrapped in baking paper, while Nurghed had a rectangular box covered in a red handkerchief. Tucked away in the knot at the top, was a small note that Nurghed chuckled at before putting it in his pocket.

"My wife goes to too much trouble at times," said Nurghed.

Seamus' wife had given up making his sandwiches after several complaints from Seamus about the mayonnaise to tuna ratio.

Man, and Orc sat back down with Marg. Nurghed unwrapped the package and all could see the trouble his wife had gone to. The lettuce was cut thinly and evenly, the carrot and cucumber were cut into stars that made a galaxy of taste and essential vitamins drizzled with mayonnaise. In a compartment beside the salad was a thin meat, marinated in a dark sauce.

"That looks delicious Nurghed, what have you brought for lunch?" asked Marg.

Nurghed smiled at his good wife's work and answered, "Asian."

"Lovely, is it chicken, or pork?"

Nurghed swallowed the tender, sweet meat he had placed in his mouth. His tusks had moved left and right as he chewed. "No, Asian. My wife buys it from a butcher in our neighborhood. It's imported through a fair-trade initiative that sells grain fed stock."

What Nurghed was saying dawned on Seamus. He had read about it of course. The '67 accords had given legal recognition to a number of Orcish traditions provided that they were undertaken with the explicit permission of all those involved. But how could an Orc get permission from a person to be willingly butchered? Horoscope be damned, how could Seamus be friends with an Orc? Stonebutter would probably go to a staff barbeque to see who was fattening up the most. Did Thomas, Arthur and Jones know that they were a potential meal for one of their employees? How would Seamus organise catering for the next staff training day? These were all thoughts that Seamus Kent would have later. Right now, there was but a single thought in Seamus' mind. A thought he uttered uncharacteristically without thinking.

"Th-th-that's cannibalism!"

Nurghed took another mouthful of human flesh, as if to suggest Seamus' accusation was hardly worth interrupting his lunch for. He wiped his mouth before answering. "Cannibalism implies that I am consuming the flesh of my own species, Mr Kent. As Orc and human are not the same in this regard, I am no more a cannibal that you are when eating a cow. What I eat now has been eaten by my kind for thousands of years, and we have come a long way to continue this tradition in the most ethical way possible. As the Non-Human Resources Manager, I thought that you would understand this."

The rest of the induction was awkward and over quickly. Man, and Orc bid each other a formal farewell before Seamus retreated to his office to work on a solution. Marg was a chatterbox and Seamus worried that this could be worse than the water cooler incident of '09. Seamus was so rattled by the event, he had three coffees before going home. How could he have been so stupid? Saying such a culturally insensitive thing eroded what faith the firm had in him and the new Non-Human Resources Manager. He set the precedent for welcoming an Orc to Thomas, Arthur and Jones Accounting and Seamus couldn't well let culturally insensitive comments be allowed in the workplace. If Seamus had a problem with another man being eaten by an Orc, then it was up to him to move past it.

If the water cooler incident of '09 had taught Seamus anything, it was that he was a steady hand on the tiller in a storm. He wrote an Orc sensitivity program, A.R.I.E.S, the All Races Integrated Empathy Strategy, in homage to Seamus' and Nurhead's first lunch together. As the first participant of A.R.I.E.S, Seamus was surprised to see that he had passed so well. Seamus offered Nurghed an apology and the opportunity for mediation. Nurghed said the apology was sufficient and man and orc shook hands.

Eventually, word reached Cecil Arthur of Nurghed Stonebutter's dining proclivities, but when Seamus Kent mentioned Stonebutter's impressive golf game, Cecil Arthur seemed happy to be more welcoming of Orcish traditions. And with a handicap of three, Nurghed Stonebutter would be a welcome addition to the Thomas, Arthur and Jones golf team.

About the Author:

A.G Jones is a dabbler in many things. When he isn't trying to encourage the next generation in his English classroom, he is writing, lost in a book, rolling D20s, or plucking the strings of his Double Bass. With a background in Comparative Religious Studies, faith, organised religion and the power of symbols are often a big part of his writing. A quiet life in regional Victoria provides A.G. Jones with plenty of time to explore new worlds of his own and others creation.

Witchfinder's Lover

Stephen Herczeg

"Good evening Miss Audrey," said William as he helped the young woman into the front seat of the small horse-drawn wagon. His bright blue eyes shone with an inner glow even in the dim afternoon light.

"Thank you, William. Damnable horrible night for it." Audrey looked up at the darkening sky and threatening clouds building on the horizon.

William sat down beside her and took up the reins. "That it is Miss Audrey. That it is. We should make good time. If it holds out, we'll be in Ipswich before midnight. If not, then there are a couple of inns along the way. Small towns but nice enough. Mr Hopkins has told me to look after you as if you were me own daughter, so nary a hair on your head will be mussed if I can helps it."

Audrey glanced around the wagon. The tiny market town of Lavenham wasn't much to look at and she was quite glad to leave.

The townsfolk weren't happy when they arrived and were even angrier now, they were going.

Granted, Matthew had executed justice on the town and found five of their women guilty of various acts of witchcraft.

Audrey Mayfair was proud of her role as chief investigator for Matthew Hopkins, the Witchfinder General. Her job was to unearth the rumours, gossip and scuttlebutt in the towns they visited and locate the practitioners of witchcraft and devil worship.

It mostly involved finding those who had been wronged in their dealings with the miscreants. Her methods ranged from bribery to seeding doubt in the minds of the townsfolk. When small minds were reminded of the commitment to their Lord, they were quick to denounce criminals in their midst.

Upon Audrey's recommendation, Matthew brought the accused to trial. The defendant was offered a choice. Confess and burn at the stake or be dunked in a lake. If the waters rejected them, they would be hanged, if not they were deemed innocent and given a proper Christian burial.

After many successes over the last few years, Audrey had come to Matthew's attention and been elevated in his ranks. Eventually, she had been raised in his affections as well, spending the last year as Matthew's lover. Even though, Matthew operated above the church and was immune to much of their prescribed doctrine. Their life together enjoyed all the characteristics of a married couple, except in the eyes of the Lord.

"Hold on Miss and we'll be away."

William's voice shook Audrey from her reveries.

She held onto the side rail as the horse kicked and the carriage jolted forward. Soon they were away from Lavenham and trotting along through open countryside.

William raised his voice over the sound of the horse's clopping, "so, you'll be joining Mr Hopkins up in Norwich?"

"Yes. We are expecting to unearth a lot of witches and Mr Hopkins wants me to bring Shelley and Caroline."

"You'll be using the closed carriage, with young Rodgers driving it, then," he said as he looked over his shoulder at the darkening sky. "Least it will keep you out of this sort of weather." He lashed the reins to spur the horse on. "Come on Nobby, you dozy mule, get a wiggle on. There's a tankard of ale waiting for me, I can feel it in me bones."

The wagon rocked and jumped over the uneven and rutted road. Audrey and William held on for dear life, crashing into each other numerous times to avoid being thrown from the seat.

A drop of rain landed on Audrey's neck and she peered over her shoulder. A dark thunderhead rolled across the fields, chasing them with outstretched arms of black cloud. The wind picked up and made desperate grabs at her hat and coat. The rain started in earnest and soon they were both drenched to the skin.

Nobby galloped on through the torrent, his steady feet finding footholds on the muddy track where none appeared to be.

Until it happened.

A bright bolt of lightning blasted down and smashed into a gigantic oak tree on the apex of a tight corner. The trunk ignited into the shape of a flaming ram's skull, with curling horns on either side, and glowing ovine eyes that stared straight into Audrey's own.

Nobby skidded away from the spectre, galloping off the road and into an adjacent gulley.

The wagon twisted sideways, launching both Audrey and William into the air. As she flew, time slowed, extending her moment of terror. The wagon crashed and the terrified horse screamed in pain at the bottom of the hollow. William landed with a bone crunching thud, and Audrey upon meeting the sodden earth, heard her leg crack as it struck a protruding rock. Her mind exploded with fire and pain as her head hit the ground.

It was extinguished as the darkness consumed her.

Audrey's eyes flickered open. A pale blur hovered nearby framed against a dark background. She blinked several times to clear the crust from her eyes. "William?" she said.

The pale figure shook its head and spoke. "No, no. I'm Maggie."

Audrey lifted a hand that felt like a dead weight and rubbed at her eyes. She blinked and peered at the figure.

"M-M-Maggie?" Audrey asked, her throat raw. "Where is William? He was driving. I saw him fly. Where am I? Is Matthew here?" The figure came into focus, and Audrey saw she was a beautiful young woman.

"You are in our house. A little way from where your carriage crashed. I don't know who Matthew is, perhaps you can tell me about him when you're a little better. As to your driver, William is it? We will talk later. You are still weak. Rest a while and I'll bring food to help build your strength up."

Audrey slumped back into the bed. She closed her eyes to seek more sleep. Voices drifted into the room.

"Well?" said a deeper, older voice.

"She has awakened but is still exhausted. She asked about William. That would be the driver I'd say. I've told her to go back to sleep. I'll take her some food in a while."

"It's a waste of our food," said a gruff voice.

"Esme, what a horrible thing to say. We have more use for that young lass than we do for the food. She will be important in the coming days," said the older voice.

Audrey's mind trailed off as sleep claimed her once more.

She awoke with a start and looked around the dark room. Her head still throbbed, and she found a huge egg-shaped lump on her forehead that was tender to touch. She winced and cried out in pain.

A noise grabbed her attention.

Moonlight filtered through the gaps in the window shutters and cast bright lines across the sheer curtain and onto the floor.

A shadow fell across the window. Audrey gasped, as she watched it sway from side to side before moving away. A crunch of gravel and a scraping noise followed its withdrawal.

Audrey sat still, her eyes fixed on the window as the crunching footsteps receded. For what seemed like an eternity, she held her breath, alert for any sign of return.

Finally, she let her breath out. She thought about looking outside but fear got the better of her. She lay down and pulled the bed covers over her head.

Bright light exploded across Audrey's closed eyelids. She turned her face away from the sunlight that streamed into the room, opened her eyes, blinked several times to adjust her focus and peered back.

Maggie stood in the middle of the open window, her arms stretched up to the ceiling welcoming the bright daylight onto her face and the green dress she wore. "Ah, nothing better than a beautiful sun-filled day," she said over her shoulder.

Audrey peered past her and spied the rolling fields stretching out toward the distant hills. Seas of long grasses and crops swayed in the light breeze and dazzled in the sunlight. "It's beautiful," she said.

Maggie turned and smiled. "It is," she said. "Today we'll get you up and about, so you can enjoy it and take your fill of the mother's gifts."

"The mother?"

"Yes, Mother Nature, silly."

Audrey mouthed a silent, "Oh" as Maggie moved across to the bed. She pulled back the covers and Audrey saw that she was now dressed in an unfamiliar plain spun smock that reached to just above her knees, and that a bandage had been wrapped around her right calf. She winced as the memory of pain spiked in her brain.

Maggie undid the binding around Audrey's leg and drew the bandage away. Audrey reeled back at the foul odour and closed her eyes to protect herself from what was sure to be a hideous sight. The young woman removed the dressing from Audrey's leg revealing long ropes of thick yellow fluid which smelt revolting. Audrey reeled back at the smell and let out a disgusted cry.

Maggie chuckled and said, "Oh, it's not as bad as all that. Esme's poultices are always a little smelly, but they do the job. See for yourself."

Audrey opened her eyes to see the thick fluid on her leg as Maggie dropped the dressing into a bucket by the bed. As Maggie gently washed away the remains of the foul-smelling poultice with a wet rag, Audrey winced, expecting more pain, but there was very little. Once clean, the devastation she expected on her leg was nothing more than a mass of dark but fading bruises.

Audrey stared in surprise. "But I heard it snap. And the pain. I was sure it was broken. How?" she stammered.

Again, Maggie chuckled. "Oh, no. It wasn't broken, just a fair bit of bruising and some small cuts. We cleaned you up, put the poultice on and bandaged it. You slept for the most part, but that looks like it's healing very nicely," she said.

Audrey was dumbstruck. "How long have I been here?"

"Just two nights. You're young. Strong. You heal quickly. Esme's poultice worked a treat as well."

Audrey was about to ask more, but Maggie reached out for her arms.

"Let's see how it holds up to some walking." She slipped Audrey forward until her feet touched the floor.

"I don't know. I don't think I should just yet."

"Nonsense, just put some weight on it and see how it goes."

Audrey placed her feet flat on the floor, leaned forward and tentatively stood up. She expected searing pain to lance up her leg, but there was none.

Maggie led Audrey with no problems. She smiled. Audrey smiled.

"Excellent, let's go out and see the others," Maggie said.

The pair stepped through into a room devoid of humans. Maggie frowned. "I thought they were here. I wanted them to finally meet you face to face," Maggie said as she moved across to another doorway and looked through.

Audrey followed Maggie into the plain but functional room. Its simplicity was in stark contrast the large ram's head carved above the door. The detail was striking, with eyes that seemed to fix on her own gaze.

Maggie suddenly pulled back from the doorway, as two men burst through carrying a third. They lifted the man and dumped him onto the table. He cried out in pain.

His lower leg was a mess of blood and torn tissue, a jagged piece of white bone stuck out of the wound. Audrey turned away with an audible gasp, but the disturbing sight dragged her attention back.

Maggie moved across to the table and patted the man's forehead, cooing to him to allay his pain. "It will be alright Sam. Gertha and Esme will be here soon. You will be fine in no time."

The man's only response was to cry out again. As he began squirming in pain, Maggie looked up at the two men. "David, Michael, hold him still. Otherwise, he'll hurt himself further."

They nodded and took Sam by the shoulders and thighs to stifle his movement.

Just then two more women entered the room, a matronly woman in her late forties and a withered old crone that must have been well past eighty. The matron held a basket of herbs and mushrooms. She went to the kitchen cupboard and placed it down.

The old crone turned to Maggie, "Maggie. Hot water and some clean cloth." She craned her ancient neck to the matronly woman. "Gertha, prepare a porter's poultice."

"Already on it, Esme." The matron pulled down a mortar and pestle and several jars of herbs and grains.

Audrey watched her as she ground and stirred up the mixture.

The crone moved across to the cupboard and pulled out a pottery jar. She extracted a couple of dried leaves and moved back to Sam. She grabbed his mouth and popped the leaves inside. "Chew on this for a bit," she said.

Sam obliged. The action of chewing tore his attention away from the pain. As he chewed, Sam's eyes rolled back as if drawn into a dream-like state. A powerful stench of strange herbs filled the room. Esme placed a small cylinder of leather into the injured man's mouth.

Esme looked at Michael. "Make sure he bites down on this while I fix his leg, he's gonna need to," she said. The man nodded and managed to hold Sam down with one hand and the leather block with the other.

Maggie arrived with the hot water and cloths. Esme dunked a cloth into the water, wrung it out and slopped it onto the leg. Sam cried out in pain, his teeth clamping down hard on the leather.

"Good boy," said Esme. "But we've only started."

"Should we get a Doctor?" Audrey asked, grabbing Maggie by the arm.

The young girl shrugged her off, a hint of smile on her face. "No Doctor can do what Esme can."

Horrified, but fascinated, Audrey watched as Esme went to work. She quickly cleaned the area around the wound, revealing the extent of the injury, then dropped the blood-soaked cloth into the bucket and prepared herself for the next stage.

"Hold him down boys. Tight," Esme said, pressing her fingers against the protruding bone and pushed it back into the wound.

Audrey gasped and clutched her hands to her face. They slipped away and folded together as she let out a silent prayer for the poor man.

Sam screamed out, the leather bite-block exploded from his mouth and landed on the floor. He struggled against Michael's hands for a moment then flopped back unconscious.

"Well that makes things easier," said Esme. She quickly pushed the two pieces of leg bone together, using her palm to finish the job. The bones ground together horribly as they slipped back in place. Bile rose in Audrey's stomach.

"Needle and yarn."

Maggie pulled out a long needle with the yarn already threaded from a nearby sewing basket. Esme pinched the skin together, grabbed the needle and sewed the wound shut. When finished, she gave the bloody needle back to Maggie.

"Gertha, poultice."

Gertha brought the mortar over and placed it on the table. Esme slopped the thick mixture across the entire area while Gertha placed wet strips of cloth across the wound, then tied them up with dry strips.

The whole process lasted less than five minutes. When finished, Esme stepped back, washed her hands in the bucket and wiped them down her apron.

She turned to the men and said, "Right, take him home. Bedrest for a couple of days. I'll see him tomorrow to check on the wound. Tell Mabel I'll expect a healthy spring lamb come April."

Michael nodded his head and said, "Thank you, Granny. Will do." The two men bowed, carefully picked up Sam and headed for the door.

Audrey simply stood in the shadows near the wall, a dumbstruck look on her face.

The crone turned towards her. "You'd be Audrey then."

Audrey lay back on the bed and digested the events of the day. Her head swam.

How did I end up here? I should be in Ipswich, ready to join Matthew in Norwich.

Her thoughts turned to Matthew.

Would he miss her yet? Would he be worried? No, too early. He'd be preparing to seek out the coven of witches.

The crone had introduced herself as Esmerelda. Granny to many, Esme to some. Esme and Gertha said they had lived on the farm for decades, Maggie only joining them the previous year. She had run away from her own parents and found solitude and safety with the two older women.

They talked for ages with Audrey, about her background, her childhood, her time with Matthew, the witch trials and various other small topics. But the three women didn't talk much about themselves. Audrey knew almost as much now as she had this morning.

When Audrey raised the subject of William, her driver, the older pair made excuses and left. Her heart sank when Maggie said they had found poor William at the scene. He had broken his neck and was beyond even Granny's healing skills. They'd buried him near the road and placed a small cross as a marker.

Audrey cried, for William, for Maureen his widow, and with the realisation that it could have so easily been her. William was a friend of Matthew's, but only a colleague to her. It was those piercing blue eyes that would remain in her mind as a reminder of him, but his face would fade with time.

Finally, Maggie led Audrey outside into the light of the day.

The farm was small. The women raised some pigs and sheep and tended a small vegetable and herb garden. They were women of limited wants and means, and the farm satisfied most of them.

During the day, a constant dribble of visitors from nearby farms and villages came to the farm. Maggie said most came because of health problems. The three women studied the healing arts and were happy to offer their services to folk. They asked for no money, but any donations of food or other items were always welcome.

All the visitors followed the path from the north, as the southern end of the farm was bordered by a deep, thick forest that stretched off into the distance. Audrey peered towards it.

Maggie noticed and said, "The wood is ancient. Filled with the power of nature. There we seek the special herbs and mushrooms for our poultices and medicines."

Audrey concentrated harder, but her eyes failed to penetrate the darkness of the trees.

"The folk around here fear the wood. Which suits us as they leave it well alone."

Audrey eyes opened wide as she caught sight of a tall, gnarled figure standing near the edge of the trees. She blinked several times, but by the time she looked back, it was gone.

I must have imagined it.

Audrey snapped awake. The last vestiges of a scraping noise died away in her subconscious. A loud clap of thunder erased any further memories.

She sat bolt upright and listened to the sounds of the night. Rain sheeted against the thatched roof of the cottage. A stiff wind blew the curtains away from the window opening. Lightning lit up the gaps in the shutters.

Audrey rose and stepped across to the window. She pushed on the shutters, but they were locked on the outside.

Strange. Why lock it from outside? It's as if to keep someone in.

She peered through the largest gap. The night was pitch black, everything outside was obscured by the driving rain, only the lightning providing brief illumination.

A sudden clap of thunder shook her to her marrow. Lightning lit up the barren hill to the north-east of the farm.

A figure, slim and small, stood naked on the summit.

She stared at the hill, waiting for another flash of lightning. It came. She saw a woman. Young, slim, lithe but muscular. Her long tresses stuck to her naked back.

Maggie?

Another flash revealed a second figure. A huge, hulking form that towered over the smaller. Its humongous claws outstretched towards the woman, ready to strike.

Audrey screamed, "Maggie, watch out!"

Another crash of thunder and the lightning showed the slim figure alone again. The woman—Maggie?—turned towards Audrey. In an instant, Audrey saw her mistake.

The figure was ancient. Its skin wrinkled and sagging. Its breasts flopped like bags of soggy meat. The thin, grey hair hung in lank clods across the scalp and shoulders.

It wasn't Maggie but Esme. Eighty-year-old Esme. Standing naked in the rain.

Her bedroom door flew open. Maggie charged in carrying a candle, her face tired but frightened by Audrey's screams. "Audrey? What's wrong? Are you alright? Is your head paining you?"

The candle threw strange shadows across the room and made the young woman look ancient.

Audrey turned and pointed at the window. "I saw Esme. In the rain. Naked. There was a beast. I was afraid for her."

Maggie peered through a gap in the shutters. Her calm façade dropped for a moment. "There's nothing there. Why would Esme be out in this foul weather? See for yourself," she said, a touch of anger in her voice.

"But I'm sure I saw someone out there. I thought it was you, but then it looked more like Esme." Audrey peered out again. The storm raged on, but there was nothing there. She turned back to Maggie, a sheepish look on her face. "I'm sorry. I must have dreamt it all."

Maggie nodded, a smile returning to her face. "That must be it. Sleep again. We can go look outside tomorrow if that would comfort you."

Audrey nodded as she climbed back into bed. She laid back and closed her eyes. As soon as Maggie stepped out of the room, she sat up and stared at the window.

The storm raged on. Lightning lit up the night. Audrey began to tire, and her lids grew heavy. She failed to notice the shadow thrown across the window by one massive sheet of lightning.

By the next flash it was gone.

Audrey shuffled into the empty living area. The sun shone bright and high in the sky outside. She spied the hill off in the distance and her mind filled with images of a naked Esme and the towering hulk lit by the storm.

Maggie's voice broke her reverie. "You're up then, sleepy head?"

Audrey turned to see the young woman enter with a basketful of fresh vegetables. She moved to the cupboard and put the basket down.

"How is your head this morning?"

After the excitement of the thunderstorm and Audrey's visions of a naked woman, she hadn't even remembered about lump on her head and the headache it had caused. The pain had reduced, but a fog remained. "It's better. I just feel a little groggy," she replied.

Maggie gathered some items and set the table with a loaf of bread, a pot of marmalade and cutlery and crockery. She placed a jug of water and cup beside them. "Here, have some breakfast. It will settle your stomach and help your head." Maggie looked around, then sat and cut herself a slice of bread and piled on some marmalade. She sat back and took a bite, her eyes closed in bliss as she ate and moaned with pleasure. "Mrs Johnstone from two farms over makes this marmalade. It is wonderful," she said pushing the pot and bread towards Audrey. A cheeky grin came to Maggie's face. "Esme and Gertha are visiting a new mother at a nearby farm, so have some before they return. It's Esme's favourite. She's very protective of it."

Audrey smiled despite herself and prepared a slice of marmalade bread. She realised how hungry she was and wolfed down the first slice in no time. Once she was halfway through a second, she began to feel much better. She looked down at the simple homespun smock Maggie had loaned her. "Do you think we could find my carriage and bring back some of my things? I'm very thankful, but don't want to impose too much," she said.

Maggie's face changed from offended to a broad smile. "Certainly," she said. "We can visit that little hillock where you thought you saw Esme as well. It's on the way."

The small hill was nothing out of the ordinary. It was more the location that made it stand out. The immediate area surrounding it was flat and low, providing Audrey with a wonderful view across the farm to the deep dark wood. Audrey shielded her eyes and peered in the opposite direction. She noticed a narrow dirt track winding off into the distance.

Maggie's voice snapped her attention. "That's where your carriage left the road, where we found you and your poor driver." Maggie pointed towards a small copse of trees with her right hand while fingering the odd amulet she wore around her neck. It was a small stone carved into a curved three-pronged triskele. In the middle was a carving in the same style of ram's head as that above the kitchen door. Audrey thought it a pretty but queer looking object.

After a short trudge across the muddy field they came upon the overturned carriage and the remains of the horse. Audrey cast an eye over the corpse of poor Nobby. The local foxes had found him and had their way. Flesh gave way to bone and sinew across the length of the animal. She turned away in revulsion and breathed deeply to maintain her composure and keep her breakfast intact.

"Poor animal," said Maggie. "It doesn't look like it suffered, and it has provided others with food, so all is not lost."

Audrey shot her a withering glance.

Maggie shrugged. "It is the way of the Mother. Of nature. Eventually we all become food for the worms." She pointed at an overturned trunk nestled against a tree. "Is that yours?"

Audrey looked over and nodded. They both made their way to the trunk. Audrey kept her back to the decimated body of the horse and swatted at several flies as they sought out fresher meat.

Maggie turned the heavy trunk over, showing a surprising amount of strength. "It doesn't look damaged."

Audrey hunkered down and unlatched it. Her clothes and possessions were all still in place, if a little mussed up from their journey down the hill. She peered back up the slope and sighed. "How will we get this up to the road? And how will we get it back to the farm?"

"Together," said Maggie, grabbing a handle with one hand and hefting her half of the trunk up with ease.

Audrey stared in disbelief for a moment then grabbed her side with both hands and managed to repeat Maggie's feat.

By the time they reached the roadside, Audrey was bathed in sweat, her smock sticking to her in several unwanted places. Maggie showed no sign of fatigue.

"How are you not sweating?" Audrey asked, but was cut off by a shout from behind. A wagon approached, driven by Sam.

The same Sam who had been lying on a table, his leg a mess of rent flesh and splintered bones, not more than a day before. He smiled, waved and shouted, "Hello there, Miss Maggie. What are you doing down here?"

Maggie waved back. "Well met, Sam. We came to collect some of Audrey's belongings from the wagon down the bank."

"Aye, nasty that was. I feel for the poor driver," he said looking across the road to a small pile of dirt marked with two sticks tied into a simple cross. It was nestled back from the road in a small clearing bordered on three sides by short flowering shrubs.

Audrey followed his gaze and saw the grave. Shock blossomed on her face. "William?" she gasped and made her way to the graveside. She knelt and the tears flowed. "Oh, William. I'm so sorry."

Maggie stepped up next to her and stood quietly to give Audrey a moment of grief. "When we found him, he was already gone, much like the horse. We thought this was the best for him," she said looking around at the beautiful surroundings.

Audrey looked up at Maggie then around the area. She slowly stood, dropped her head and said, "Thank you. I think he would have liked this place."

A torrent of tears spilled forth again. Maggie placed an arm around Audrey and brought her face to her shoulder. Sam stepped up next to the pair, removed his hat and dropped his head slightly in deference to the dead man.

After a while, Audrey's tears subsided, and she pulled away. She took one last look at the grave and moved towards the wagon.

"I've loaded the trunk and can take the two of you home, if you'd like," Sam told Maggie.

Audrey climbed up into the wagon, her heart heavy with sorrow for poor William. She looked back towards the grave and vowed to come back and pay her respects once more before leaving the farm.

Audrey watched, astounded, as Sam carried her heavy trunk in from the wagon. He strode past the table where, only the day before, he'd writhed in agony as Granny Esme pushed the exposed pieces of his leg bone back together and bound his gaping wound. There was no limp. No wobble in his stride. Just a confident man full of health.

Maggie stopped him and told him to sit up on the table. He duly complied and stretched his leg out for her.

She unbound the bandages and Audrey expected to see a bleeding, weeping wound with puckered skin, but was astonished to see that the leg was healed. The flaps of skin sealed back together with a slight ridge where they joined.

Maggie smiled. "That's healed nicely."

"You can thank Granny for that. A miracle worker if you ask me," said Sam.

Audrey remained silent. Her eyes wide in shock.

Was this magic? Real magic?

Maggie cleansed the remains of the poultice away from the Sam's wound and went to fetch some instruments to remove the stitches.

Audrey took her chance. "Has this happened before?" she asked Sam.

He smiled. "Oh, yar, Granny Esme and Mother Gertha have been helping us folk for years. They never ask for much but when we is sick or injured, they do what they do and pretty soon we're right as rain again."

"Is it magic?"

Sam looked a little puzzled by the question, then brightened. "I don't think so. They always use ointments and such like. They don't do no spells or naught. So, I wouldn't call it magic. They are magical I suppose, but t'ain't magic."

As Maggie returned, Audrey stepped away and fell silent.

"I heard voices, what were you two talking about?"

"Nothing much Miss, just a bit of this an' that."

Maggie eyed him for a moment then set about removing the stitches. Sam winced a couple of times but remained silent.

When finished, Maggie stood up, gathered the discarded bandages and stitching and took them away.

Audrey spoke quietly to Sam, "The ladies have been wonderful in helping me recover, but I feel I've encroached on their kindness quite enough. Would you be so kind as to take me into the nearest sizeable town? From there I should be able to find someone to take me to Ipswich. I really must be getting back."

"Oh, aye, that should be fine. I can probably take you now, if you'd like. Or in the morning if you want to be having your goodbyes," he said.

Audrey was about to speak when Maggie returned. She stared at Sam and raised an eyebrow. Sam's demeanor changed completely.

"I . . . I just realised I won't be able to take you for a while. I'll be out for the next few days. I've got to go north and help out at my brother's farm." He replaced his hat, shifted towards the door and bid Maggie goodbye. "Thanking you again, Miss Maggie. You, Granny and Mother Gertha. Thank you again. We've started fattening up one of the lambs ready to bring across to you in a month or so." Sam almost collided with the door frame in his hurry to exit.

Audrey watched him go then turned back to Maggie, a look of severe disappointment on her face. "How?" she said.

"How what?" Maggie answered.

Audrey studied her for a moment before replying. "How did his leg heal so quickly? There's no way on God's Earth it could have healed by itself in such a short time."

"It may be that the problem lies is in your choice of God."

"What do you mean? There's only one God"

"Some think that, but we do not follow the teachings of the carpenter's son. Our Gods were here long before him and will be here long after he has faded from the memories of man."

Audrey's eyes opened with her mind. "Witches," she said. "You are witches."

Maggie grimaced at the name. "That is a name ascribed to us in Christ's book. A foul name but not of our choosing. We know no name. We are just as we are." She pointed towards the carving above the doorway. "Our Gods are old. They draw their power from the Earth. We seek that power from Lord Atho, the old god of the forests. We are his children. We harness the power of Atho and of Hecate, the mother, to heal the sick and lame. Much like the stories of the Carpenter, but his power was attributed to a higher being. Truth be told he was more like us than not."

Audrey was affronted by the accusation. "Blasphemy. You're saying Jesus was a witch," she spat.

"That or a fraud. Perhaps his lover, the Magdalene, was one of my sisters and performed the miracles in his stead. Stranger things have happened through the ages."

"Enough!" shouted Audrey. "I'm leaving. This is insane. I will bring Matthew Hopkins the Witchfinder General to this place, to rain his judgement down on you all." She strode to the door of her bedroom. A final rebuff came to her mind and she stopped to address Maggie once more.

As Audrey turned, she was shocked to find the witch standing close behind. She opened her mouth to speak but Maggie raised a hand and blew yellow powder into her face.

Audrey was in darkness when she awoke. Moonlight filtered through the shuttered window. She sat upright; the fog of her dreams still bound her mind in a cloud of murkiness.

Was it all a dream? Am I still in Lavenham? Am I in Ipswich?

The murmur of the three women's voices filtered through from next door. Flickering candlelight seeped into the room from the base of the door. "It must be tonight. The moon is high. The night is still," said Esme.

"I'm so sorry. I lost my temper. She won't come willingly now like we planned," said Maggie's softer voice.

"Foolish child. It doesn't matter. Once Hecate possesses her, it won't matter how upset she is," said Gertha.

What do they mean 'once Hecate possesses her'?

Audrey backed away from the door and stared at it in shock. A chill ran up her spine. The three women had healed her only for their own means. Hecate. Maggie had mentioned Hecate. She'd also heard it called out by many of Matthew's accused. That was their god or their demon.

They mean me harm. They want to sacrifice me to this Hecate. I must get away. I must find Matthew.

She spied her trunk and pushed it against the door to stop it from opening. The scraping noise was a deadly cacophony in the quiet room.

"What was that?" Gertha shouted.

"She's awake," cried Esme.

Audrey spun for the window and pushed at the shutters. Behind her, there was a thump at the door. The shutters were locked tight. A crack of light appeared as the door was inched open.

"No," she cried and pushed again. The shutters bulged outwards but held fast. She kicked them. Only pain greeted her.

Another thump echoed through the room. The crack was wider as the heavy trunk was forced back.

Audrey spied a thin rod of metal in the gap between the shutters.

The bolt outside has been thrown.

She pushed her fingers into the gap and tried to move the rod. It jiggled in its holder.

Another thump. Maggie's face appeared at the crack.

"Audrey. Stop. It's not what you think. We mean you no harm. We only want you to help us."

Audrey concentrated on the bolt. She jammed her hand though the shutter and wrapped a finger around it. Finally, it slid out from the bracket. She flung the shutters open. A cry behind her and Maggie squeezed into the room followed by Gertha. Audrey sensed freedom and turned back to the window.

Standing before her was a demon from Hell. The hulking form she'd spied on the hill. A giant covered in a coat of coarse dark wool. It's long, pointed face stared down at her with two great ram's horns curled on either side of its head.

Audrey backed away at the sight. A scream caught in her throat. As she turned away, her gaze were drawn to the creature's eyes. Sparkling through the gloom like diamonds made flesh were the palest blue eyes she had ever seen. Eyes so alien in this beast's head, nestled under the thick brow within a cowl of dark wool.

Her terror faded as realisation dawned in her mind. Those eyes. She had seen those eyes so many times but in another's face.

William?

"Oh, William? What have they done you?" she said.

Suddenly, William's monstrous face disappeared as a thick sack was thrust over her head. Stars exploded across her mind as pain erupted in the side of her head. As the darkness closed in, she heard the women argue.

"You didn't have to hit her," said Maggie.

"Much easier to handle this way," said Gertha.

"That was foolish, I just hope you haven't damaged her. Hecate won't be pleased," said Esme.

"You can always fix her up afterwards," said Gertha.

"True that," answered Esme.

The flickering flames of an oil burner atop an iron tripod cast dancing shadows and light upon the thick canopy of branches and leaves above. The sweet smell of the oil pervaded the underlying odour of rotting leaves and mulch. Audrey found herself in a clearing surrounded by a thick, dark border of trees. She realised she was inside the forest near the witches' farmhouse.

"She awakes." Esme's gravel voice echoed across the area.

Maggie, naked except for her triskele amulet and a daisy chain in her hair, stepped into Audrey's view. She smiled a placating smile. "Welcome back Audrey. It is time for you to join us."

"No," Audrey said weakly. She tried to raise her hands. They were bound as were her legs. She, too, was naked and lying on a rough and cold stone slab. A ram's skull stared back at her from the end of the altar.

Esme and Gertha stood naked to one side. On the other side, partially hidden in the trees, was the hulking form that had caused Audrey to faint.

Esme turned and motioned to it. "Lord Atho. Come forth. Your bride awaits."

The beast stepped into the light and stood to its full height. Audrey gasped. William's bright blue eyes peered out from each side of the long ovine face. Two large curled horns grew on each side of his head, their tips ending in sharp points jutting forward of his brow.

The creature stood seven feet tall with a light covering of dirty brown wool. To Audrey, it looked like an overstuffed sack, as if the beast beneath was too large for its own skin. The beast walked forward with an awkward gait. The body fighting against the actions of the mind.

Oh, William, thought Audrey as she stared at the possessed and corrupted body of her once proud friend.

Lightning split the sky. Thunder cracked through the silence. The Horned God stood and reached towards the sky beyond. Power leapt up from the ground and into his form. The muscles in his arms and legs rippled and grew, straining further against the tautness of his skin.

His barrel chest expanded and filled his lungs to feed the fire within. He bellowed, either in pain or triumph.

Atho stepped next to Audrey. She gasped and tried to pull away from him, turning her head aside.

Esme appeared on that side of the altar. Her sagging skin and breasts providing only a slightly more palatable view. The old woman held a short bone-handled knife and a carved stone triskele similar to Maggie's, complete with a ram's head at its centre. She placed the triskele on Audrey's chest and before Audrey could reel back, touched it with the tip of the knife.

Sparks flew through Audrey's body and she could only move her head to one side. There, she spied Atho's bright blue sparkling eyes.

Esme raised her face skywards. "Hecate. We have prepared a vessel for your entry into this world."

Thunder cracked outside the forest and lightning shone through the gaps in the canopy.

"Hecate. Your King awaits. This vessel is ripe for your taking. Come now and claim her for your own. Then cleanse this world of those that would destroy your servants."

Audrey cried out, "William. William, I know you're still in there. I can't save you, but you can still save me. It's what Matthew would want. It's what he asked you to do."

The great horned beast drew back from the altar. Its clawed hands grasped at its head and an anguished cry left its lips and filled the clearing.

Esme turned towards the beast. "Atho, my Lord, ignore this petulant child. Your Queen will arrive soon. You will be together again in flesh."

The beast tore its hands away for a moment and looked at Esme then Audrey. Its eyes sparkled brightly in the firelight.

"Fight it William. Fight it."

The Horned God howled and grasped at its head.

Gertha stepped up to the altar. "Be quiet child. Your friend is no match for the Horned God. He who walked this world when man still swung from the trees."

"Fight it William. You are winning. Fight!" Audrey cried.

Gertha slapped her across the face. Audrey yelped; a spray of blood splattered the altar.

The great beast stopped and turned towards Audrey's cry. The eyes sparkled electric blue. It let out a terrible roar and stepped forward, swiping Gertha out of the way and sending her flying across the clearing. She slammed into a tree with a resounding crack, slid to the base, and lay still.

"No," shouted Maggie. She ran towards the horned God and beat her tiny fists against its back. "You killed Gertha. Why?"

The beast rounded on her, one thrashing arm sent Maggie's thin frame sailing over the altar and toppling into the oil burner. The oil sprayed Maggie and the surrounding grass. Flames engulfed the young girl, setting her hair ablaze and spreading across her skin. She scrambled to her feet and ran from the clearing, a bright trail of flame in her wake. The grass caught alight and fire ignited across the clearing.

The thunder and lightning raged above the forest adding a strobe effect to the bright yellow of the inferno within.

"No, you've broken the spell," Esme screamed. She stared at the hulking beast for a moment before raising her knife. "Hecate will not come if you cannot fight the man inside you. Atho you must have control."

The great beast bellowed in rage, grasping at his head as the two halves of his nature fought against each other.

Esme looked at the broken body of Gertha, at the fire encroaching on the entire clearing and back at her knife. She peered up at the beast's back and nodded to herself. "There is nothing left but to start again." She stabbed the knife deep into his back.

The beast howled in pain.

"William, no!" shouted Audrey.

The beast turned. Tried to reach for the knife, but the blade stuck deep, just out of reach. Blood poured down its back. It roared its anguish.

William grabbed the frail figure of Esme in one gigantic paw and squeezed. The old witch cried in pain. Her eyeballs bulged with the pressure.

"No, great God Atho, no. I am your servant. Fight the puny human within, or Hecate cannot return," she pleaded.

The beast reached up with his other hand, grabbed Esme around the chest and pulled. The ancient witch tore in half, spraying the burning grass with her life blood.

The thunder reached a crescendo and went silent. The night beyond the forest turned dark. The magic was gone.

The Horned God turned and stepped towards Audrey. He stumbled and dropped to one knee. He reached back and tried to grasp the knife to no avail. Behind him the flames started to take hold of the trees surrounding the clearing.

"William. The fire. We must get out of here," Audrey cried.

William regained his feet and staggered towards Audrey. He managed to slide a long vicious claw under one of the bindings. It gave way with the slightest tug; within seconds she was free.

The beast held out his hands to Audrey. All around the clearing, the fire raged as it took hold of the grass and raced up the trees. The leafy canopy was alive with fire.

Audrey climbed into the beast's hands and he turned towards the nearest gap. The fire bit into his feet and soon his lower body was bathed in flame. He howled but trudged forward holding his prize before him.

As they reached the edge of the flaming clearing, William tripped and fell. Audrey was thrown from his hands. She landed on a dry patch of dirt and rolled into the darkness, then staggered to her feet.

William, her friend, in that horribly distorted body was ablaze, his hands held out before him in a last heroic gesture. Her hero. Her protector. His duty fulfilled.

A tear sprouted from her eye and slid down her cheek.

She turned away and made for the starlight filtering through the edge of the forest. Once clear, she dropped to her knees, bowed her head and cried tears of relief and pain.

A sudden noise grabbed her attention. A dark figure moved against the bright orange background of the burning forest.

Audrey stood and stepped backwards. "William?"

The figure moved slowly forward. Audrey stared closer and it came into focus. "Maggie?"

The flaming oil had destroyed the girl. Her hair was gone. Her face a melted miasma of liquefied skin and flesh. She stopped a few paces from Audrey. Her mouth moved but failed to make any noise.

Audrey leaned closer.

"We meant no harm," Maggie whispered. "We are only here to heal. To help. Never to destroy. We only sought protection from those who would destroy us." She sucked in a lungful of air, the breath rattling in her fire-ravaged throat. "This was wrong. Esme was wrong to do this."

She brought her hand up and opened it. The melted skin split and bled with the effort. The triskele amulet sat in the middle of her black and cracked palm. The eyes of the ram, holding whatever moonlight it could capture, shone brightly against the gloom.

"Take this. It will protect and hide you from our enemies. Matthew Hopkins is wrong. He kills innocent old ladies. He cannot see the true servants of Lord Atho and Lady Hecate. He cannot see the true meaning of magic. He cannot see the truth."

Audrey picked the amulet out of Maggie's palm and stared into her eyes.

"Spread the word. Spread the truth. We only seek to help. We do not deserve to die," she whispered, then fell forward with a sickening thud.

Audrey tried to turn her over, but Maggie's skin sloughed off in her hands. She reared away in disgust. There was no helping the young woman now.

The amulet felt heavy in her hand. She opened her fingers and saw sparks flash across the surface and into her hand. There was power in it. The power of nature. The power of truth.

Audrey looked out of the carriage window as the dirty, poverty-stricken streets of Ipswich passed by. A light rain washed the worst of the stench away. Urchins played in the mud and effluent coursing its way down the ruts of the roadway. Their mothers watched from the nearby doorways; most held another babe in arms.

These are the people most in need of help. Not persecution for seeking aid from so-called witches. These are the people Maggie, Esme and Gertha would have gone out of their way to help. To nurture. To protect.

She gazed over at Matthew beside her, staring at his profile. Handsome. Confident. Committed to his cause. To seek out those he believed to be witches. To break their spirits and bodies until they confessed to their accused crimes.

"You've achieved so much. Do you still need to pursue more?" she asked.

A flash of anger ran across his face before it resumed its impassive expression. They'd held this conversation many times since Audrey's return. It was only because they headed to another mass-trial that she brought it up again. "Witchcraft is blasphemy in the eyes of the Lord. It is my God given duty to root it out and bring the accused to justice. We have talked about this enough. You have your own duties to God in this. Do you wish to cast aside all the gravitas that your responsibilities bring you?" He smiled, a lascivious smile. A smile that once caused Audrey to tingle in certain places and yearn for his touch. Now that smile only brought a feeling of disgust. A feeling she hid behind fake smiles and pleasant expressions.

"I think you are wrong," she said. "Those you accuse are simple old widows and spinsters. There is nothing blasphemous about them.

They merely help the poor unfortunates with the troubles of their simple lives."

"You accuse me of false justice?"

"Rather, misplaced justice."

His eyes drilled into her the same way he had faced down tough old ladies and driven them into snivelling messes.

Audrey held firm. She knew the reality. She knew the truth. A simple look would not bow her will or resolve.

"I think you had better watch your tongue. You speak like many of the accused before they are brought to justice. One day it may be you who stands before me. Have you thought about that?"

Audrey sat straight up. The time had come. "Yes. Yes, I have." She thumped on the roof of the carriage and shouted above the din of the horses, "Rodgers, please stop the carriage."

They slowed down. Matthew's expression grew puzzled. "What are you doing?"

The carriage drew to a stop. Audrey opened the door.

Before she could leave, Matthew grasped her arm. "Where are you going?"

"If you will not be swayed, then it is time I left. My future lies not with you. I will not be a part of this charade anymore." She tugged her arm from his grasp and hopped down from the carriage.

Matthew poked his head through the window. "You will regret this, Audrey. If you help the blasphemers, I will find you. I will bring you to justice."

Audrey smiled and watched the carriage disappear around the next corner. She drew the triskele amulet out of her small purse and gently placed it around her neck. "I doubt it," she said. Bright blue sparks ran down the ram's horns along the three spiral arms and across her chest. She shivered with the feeling. "Now to find others and spread the truth," she said.

About the Author:

Stephen is an IT Geek, writer, actor, film maker and Taekwondo Black Belt based in Canberra Australia. He has been writing for over twenty years and has completed a couple of dodgy novels, sixteen feature length screenplays and dozens of short stories and scripts.

Stephen's scripts, TITAN, Dark are the Woods, Control and Death Spores have found success in international screenwriting competitions with a win, two runner-up and two top ten finishes.
His horror stories have featured in various anthologies including: Sproutlings; Hells Bells; Trickster's Treats #1, #2 and #3; Shades of Santa; Below the Stairs; Behind the Mask; Beyond the Infinite; Beside the Seaside; The Body Horror Book; Anemone Enemy; Petrified Punks; Beginnings; Sea of Secrets, Demonic Carnival; Deep Space; A Tribute to H.G. Wells; What If?; Through Death's Door and Coffins and Dragons.

Over forty of his drabbles have been accepted by Blood Song Books; Black Hare Press; Fantasia Divinity and ThingsInTheWell.

Several of his Sherlock Holmes pastiches have been accepted for inclusion in anthologies published by Belanger Books and MX Publishing.

You can catch Stephen at his Facebook page:
https://www.facebook.com/stephenherczegauthor

WORMHOLE

Sam M. Phillips

Push ahead,

Dread wormhole,

Impetuous soul,

Driving towards her goal,

Roll ship,

Dip into slipstream,

World of colours, a dream,

Beam of light to pierce the void,

Obstacle of reality to avoid,

Devoid of substance,

Dance of molecules,

Fools and madmen tread lightly,

Brightly lit inside,

No way to hide

From choices,

These voices

Judging the forces

Which push her forward,

Toward the end,

Send word back:

The way's clear,

Attack.

About the Author:

Sam M. Phillips is the co-founder of Zombie Pirate Publishing, producing short story anthologies and helping emerging writers. His own work has appeared in dozens of anthologies and magazines such as Full Metal Horror and World War Four. He recently published his debut novella, SCIENCE FICTION DOUBLE FEATURE: Phosphorus & Into The Eye, available now!

MADE

Zena Shapter

Niam

Around the fire, in the night, with drums beating, I sit on my throne of wood and bone and grip its smooth armrests, pushing my heels into soil as warm as wounds. Orange flames whip at the black night, glowing over my tribe as they leap and twist, banging their bare blood-stained shoulders to the rhythm . . . *my* rhythm.

Not so long ago, I was the uneasy one in the corner, wary of my king. Now they all cower from me—even the warriors—and when I command them to dance, they dance. Their chants fill the air while feet stamp dirt, sending billows of dust into crackling fire until the air smells of burnt earth, and I am left amazed at why they don't challenge me. I am merely a man, same as them. I am their king, but only just. I am strong, though weakened in this moment, more than they must realise. So I take up my chalice and sip at the honey wine we seized today from our enemies, and relish both its sweet taste and my victory . . . while it lasts.

Beyond the blaze of the celebration sits a yellow grass plain. No one can see it in the dark, but it is there and, as of today, it is mine. Beyond that plain there is a stream, and beyond that a mountain. After today, those are mine too. Behind this village is a forest and a path that leads down to the sea. In every direction, as far as my eye can see, I am king now—a king taking a deep breath, easing back into his throne, and wondering what comes next. What lays beyond my sight, beyond the mountain and the seas . . . the stars beyond Serein even? I have often wondered what awaits out there, what tomorrow will bring me.

Tomorrow I shall of course demand my tribe haul the salvages we seized from our enemies and take it to the place the gods call their landing pad. When they descend from the sky in their silver beast, they will see how grateful I am for today's victory, for the wrath they gave me to make it so, and they will stare into the eyes of my tribe and entrance them all to follow me for another moon. The gift of mesmerism is the price they pay for whatever 'old tech' we kings can salvage from across our lands.

What comes after that though, given I have so much more wrath to share? Today was only the start . . .

"Niam," my brother whispers, easing close. He hasn't yet washed, so the smell of battle sweat and blood is thick and sticky on him.

I wait, then nod to indicate he may continue speaking.

"Ule has done as you wished." Bowing, he holds out the dagger of my vanquished enemy, covered in the blood that proves my son has done as I commanded.

I take the dagger and admire its balance. Its weight is perfect. I wish I could see the body myself, witness the proof that my boy is now a man, but I cannot move. Victorious as I am, under my clothes my body shakes. No matter how fierce the fire crackles and burns, I feel cold. If I were to stand now, I might collapse. The legs that served me well today on the battlefield now ache like an old man's, and in places, throb as if the flesh has been sliced down to the bone.

In places, it probably has.

So for now I don't stand. I concentrate on breathing, slowly until my shaking stops; I breathe in my reign . . . slowly so it lasts. I replaced our last king a mere moon ago, when he showed weakness. He had been king himself only a year. My reign will last longer and be more glorious. It will because it must. I have more battles to fight, more darkness to alight.

Indeed, it matters not that dancing warriors glare at me now, as they move with apparent abandon to drumbeats. They may search for weakness, as I once did, they will not find it easily. In an hour my legs will be strong again, and tomorrow, after my tribute to the gods, my power will be greater. I am not afraid of these men. I am the leader they need, a monster, a killer—just let them try.

Across the fire, in the night, I search instead for my son, Ule.

Flying embers dance across black air and lead me to his face, a man's face, aglow in the flames, watching his king. His chin low, one hand on each knee, he looks like he wants to kill me himself. Over time I will teach him how to channel that rage, as I have taught myself. There has always been this war; there will always be a war. A death on our side begets a death on theirs, and so it goes on. Ule will soon learn that what happened to his sister wasn't my fault; that what I did to him was for his own good. One day, his mother will understand too. I did it for them.

Across the fire, in the night, I see my wife dangle an arm around Ule's shoulder. When his focus does not shift, she whispers in his ear. Turning, he smiles at her and, as their eyes meet, they laugh. I can hear their laughter in my memory, though have not heard it in my ears for a long time.

It's amazing how long it has been.

Too long?

How different our lives have would been if I'd listened to her when she tried to warn me, before what happened with Lana . . . I would have more than wrath and regret for company. We would still be a family.

A family. Could that be what comes next? If only that were possible. War is one thing, but the way my son used to laugh is another.

I blink, long and with purpose, remembering.

The air fuzzes.

The very next second I am living a different life, another chance, dancing around the fire myself, in the night, with drums beating, this time alongside my boy, who is not yet a man. I may not be a king, but to Ule I am a god—at least that's how he looks at me with his eyes shining, face smiling, and his laughter, gentle yet playful like the rippling of a stream.

Beside us, my wife and daughter dance, drinking the honey wine our current king seized today from our enemies. Our cousin lost his life in battle, though I try not to think about that. The deaths are getting closer. I want to push it all away. Yet what can one man do? Our king has his reasons for battling on, for refusing any peace or truce. Moons ago, he lost loved-ones to the fighting. I can only imagine what that did to him. Just watching the danger creeping ever closer makes me fume. This is my family. I must protect them.

I lead my wife away from the fire so we can sit and watch our children dance, breathing in their laughter like air, feeling lucky to hear it. Tomorrow we must scavenge for more of what the gods call salvage, technology from the time before memory, scattered across our lands. The more salvage we gift to them when they descend in their silver beast, the more powerful our king will be and the further we can push death from our village. At least for this night our children are both safe and happy. It is a time for celebration, so celebrate we do.

Until Ule spins around so fast he falls into us, knocking wine from my wife's hand.

He laughs at his own foolishness.

"Why do you laugh at this?" I ask, standing. Does he not realise the danger around him?

"It's okay, Niam," my wife whispers, tugging my arm.

But I can't have our son being so careless. Carelessness like that could get him killed—on the battlefield, or here. What if he'd fallen into our king? "Do you think *this* funny?"

Ule straightens and stops smiling, sensing I'm serious.

Though already a woman, my daughter Lana doesn't realise. "Yes!" she laughs, bumping into me and spilling my wine too.

"Niam . . ." my wife says, staring at my clenched fist.

I try to control myself but it's hard. Why can't my children see how dangerous the village is becoming? If they don't learn respect, our king will want to teach them and he won't be as merciful as me.

I shake wine from my hand and think how best to explain. But when I hear my son and daughter sniggering, all thoughts abandon me. There is only wrath.

"This is not funny!" I yell, gripping Lana's arms and shaking her. I turn to grab Ule too, but he pushes me first.

"Get away from her!" he yells, standing in front of his sister.

It gives me the excuse I need and I drag him away. "Then you will take the lesson for both of you."

Lana cries, yelling after me—something about my being a monster, about wanting to leave the village forever.

My wife catches up to me, grabs my arm and wrenches Ule free of my grasp. "You're just like him," she hisses, gesturing at our king. "Go back to the celebration, Ule. In the morning, your father will apologise. Keep going the way you are," she warns me, "and you'll lose everything you hold dear."

She doesn't understand—I'm trying to teach our children how to survive.

The next morning though, around a weak fire, my heart beating, I search for Lana. She is not in her bed, my wife cannot find her, neither can I.

MADE

I am too harsh on my children. I love them so much. I will never again touch either of them. It was a mistake. I will control the darkness in me, my outbursts, my temper.

We race around the village, the beach, the yellow grass plains . . . Lana is nowhere. She's run away.

"This is all your fault!" my wife screams, tears streaming down her face. "She's as brash as her father!"

I say nothing, knowing she's right. Born under the same moon, it's in our nature.

By the stream, near the battlefield where our enemies were retrieving their dead last night, we find a torn corner of fabric. It resembles Lana's clothing and is covered in blood.

"No!" my wife sobs, sinking to her knees.

Our enemies have taken an opportunity and brought death closer.

And so it will go on . . . If only I hadn't lost my temper.

I blink, long and with purpose, full of regret.

The air fuzzes.

The very next second I am living a different life, another chance—it is night again, and I am standing around the village fire while drums beat and my wife warns me of my future. Ule has just bumped into her and I'm still trying to control myself, fists clenched. Do they think this funny?

"Sit back down, Niam," she mutters, "or you will become just like him." She gestures at our king. "Is that what you want?" And she tells me how monsters are made, that they fail to control their nature.

They act before they think, then have only regret and wrath as company.

As I listen, I see imaginings from a future I do not want and feel the rage ease. I don't want to hurt, or lose, my children. I want my wife to always whisper in my ear and make me laugh. So I let her pull me back down beside her, unclench my fists, and together we watch our children dance. Wine spills, but not their blood. They are safe and happy.

Still, I cannot live like this anymore, this village is baiting my fury.

So I take a deep breath, and decide. Gods or no gods, tomorrow we pack.

Leaving is what one man can do.

Lana

I wait until my mother and father think I'm dancing once more, until my brother Ule is surrounded by others, then I leave. It's only a matter of time before my father loses control and I will not wait for when he does. I saw him tonight, fists clenched, boiling on the brink. He burns hot, hunting for a way to unleash his rage. He's a monster waiting to be made. He thinks we should all fear our king, yet he is the one I fear. So I run across the yellow grass plains, away from everything I know, and sprint until I reach the stream.

There I slow, though only to hitch my skirt and focus my footing. Stars beaming brilliant above light my wade across the water. Currents cool my careful feet, hot from running, dirty with soil and grass. On the opposite bank, I go to run again, but a warm breeze brings the beating of drums. I turn to see the distant glow of our village fire, its smoke scented with burnt earth. My father knows how dangerous the village is becoming yet will never leave – my mother says it's because he can't. The gods have looked into his eyes, deep into the eyes of our whole tribe, and entranced them all to follow our king to the death. She and I are the only ones impervious to their stares.

"This is the only way I'll ever be safe," I mutter, looking skywards to gain direction.

"Safe from what?"

I jump at the voice, spin around to search for a source. Stars shine enough to light blades of grass on the riverbank, boulders upstream, and outlines of mountain peaks in the night beyond. Yet there is no one, no animal even, nearby. Did I hear a voice at all?

Water babbles softly.

Wind plays with my hair before passing.

I recognise a nearby ridge. I'm further west than I thought. Today's battle was fought near here, which means our enemies could still be close. I edge back towards the water. I should have been more careful. I've been too brash. My mother says I often act before I think, just like him. She says it's in our nature, born as we are under the same moon.

"Are you lost?" the voice comes again.

This time I turn to see a man standing on a boulder beside the stream. His beard covers as much of his face as his yellow war paint, the colour of our enemies. Metal glints at his belt.

I stumble backwards. My foot twists on uneven ground and I fall onto the bank. When I go to stand, my ankle gives way.

"Stop," the man says, jumping off the boulder.

The sound of him striding closer makes me scramble into a crawl.

"Stop!" He catches my skirt underfoot to anchor me still. "Who are you?" He leans to peer at my face. "One of them?" He gestures at the distant fire.

I breathe steadily to stay calm, nod, then think better of it. "But no more," I add.

"What do you mean, *no more*?"

"I ran away."

He straightens up and reaches for his dagger. "That is not possible. The gods assured me it wasn't." He glances behind him, listening to the night.

I say nothing; keep still. Only kings can speak with the gods, when they descend in their fearsome machines to look into the eyes of our tribes. If this warrior has spoken to the gods, he must be Eirlu, king of our enemies, ruler of a tribe entranced to be as angry as ours.

I should have said I was lost.

"I—"

"Shh!" he snaps, looking over his other shoulder, his dagger ready. "Are you alone? Don't lie! Who's with you?"

"No one!"

"Then what are you doing here?"

"I told you, I'm lost."

"No, that's not what you said before." He grabs my arm. Half lifting, half dragging, he hauls me to a boulder. He searches around, then leans close. "How did you leave them?"

My breath catches. What does he want to hear? "I, I waited until no one was looking and then . . ."

"No, I mean how *could* you."

I shake my head, confused. "My mother wanted me to be safe. In the village, there is only anger. All the deaths . . . I thought it safer out here."

"So you just . . . left? You didn't feel any need to stay." He rubs his chin, "to follow your king?"

I shake my head.

"No, no, this isn't right," he mutters. "This isn't right. You are to follow your king to the death, as my tribe is to follow me, and the other tribes are to follow their kings. The gods told me you cannot simply leave." His grip on my arm tightens. "I should kill you now."

"No, please! I'll look into their eyes again! I made a mistake, I'll make it right."

"No. *They* will." Finding his solution, he falls to my feet and rips my skirt, using his dagger to cut off a corner. Then he slices the shin of my leg.

I scream.

He clamps my mouth with a hand that tastes of dirt and death. Air invades my wound, stinging and throbbing. I reach to grip at the gash, but he pushes my hands away and holds the ripped corner of fabric to my blood until it's soaked. Then, while I rock myself in pain, he pierces the bloody cloth onto the branch of a nearby bush.

"You never ran away," Eirlu says, grabbing my arm again. "I *took* you, understand? To incite your tribe to fight. Say you understand, or I will kill you myself tonight."

"I understand."

"Good. Now come, for we have gods to meet. They *will* grant me greater power for this contravention," he mutters, dragging me into the night.

131

Niam

Around the fire, in the night, with drums beating, I paint my face red. Long have I waited to unleash the darkness within; now tonight there is nothing more my wife can say. She may predict her futures again and again, and I may have my many imaginings, rethink my actions, try to change; but it is no use, for I am who I am. Last night I controlled my temper with Ule. I let the rage ease and sat back down.

This morning Lana was missing anyway, a bloody scrap of her dress found by the stream.

There is no future now worse than this. So tomorrow I will scavenge lives, not salvages.

Spear in hand, I set off towards where the gods land in their silver beast. There I will pray for my fury tomorrow to be great.

Stars beaming brilliant above light my wade across the water. The gods' landing pad sits in open land between our village and that of our enemy. Lana probably came this way last night to pray at the pad herself. I think about the hand that caused her blood to spill and grip my spear tighter. At the pad, I approach the silver altar where tiny specks glow blue and green. Kneeling, I present my offering, a metal board the colour of grass, dotted with tiny silver squares, black lines between them. It is my apology for doubting the gods' righteousness, for even considering leaving the village. I should never have provoked their anger. Lana's demise is my punishment. My retribution will be in their glory.

"Hear me, oh gods," I say, "grant me the anger to seek my vengeance, cloud my vision with wrath."

Gods speak only to kings; but I do not need them to answer me, merely to hear. I tell them of my love for Lana and the reckoning I now deserve. As I pray, I cannot know if they listen, yet feel as if they do. There is a tightening inside me, a tension in my muscles that wasn't there before, a focus in my mind. I visualise faces I do not know and swinging fists into them. Each whack frees more fury. As my knuckles collide with imagined skin, I feel myself float, slipping into a trance, and in that intoxication I sense the gods telling me something.

When I hear footsteps, and voices with the accent of my enemies, I realise what meaning the gods speak . . . My king is weak, for it was under his rule that Lana was taken. I have come here to pray for justice, yet the gods are giving me more. Our village needs a stronger leader, bold and determined, outspoken and brash. The men now approaching are a gift—a sign of what the gods want me to do. My rage will not have to wait until morning. Tomorrow is already here.

So I hide behind the altar, balancing the weight of my spear in one hand while in the other I clench my dagger. I focus my fury. My vengeance will not stop at these few, it will weed out the weakness that brought it into being. After I am done here I will seek out our king and teach him what his weakness has meant for me.

Finally the voices are so close I can make out angry words demanding answers from the gods, demanding greater power. I raise my spear, stand, and hurl it. One of the warriors falls but there are three more. In a haze, I stab bodies, slice and cut them until they are on the ground moaning. I turn my dagger inside stomachs until warm liquid oozes thick over my arms. I move with a speed I never knew I had, and don't stop until their moans are no more.

Victorious, I thank the gods for the wrath they have given me this night, and pray they grant me more.

More wrath—more power—more focus. For I have more blood to spill, more battles to fight.

As I pass over the stilled bodies, the gods answer my prayer, sending me reason for the rage I sought.

Two of the bodies are old, elders of our enemies, and one is in royal garb.

The last body is a woman and when I recognise the fabric of her skirt—bloody like the corner of it we found by the stream this morning—I fall to my knees and moan as if I too have been stabbed.

In my craze, I did not see how close my enemies were bringing death to me. Last night, my wife tried to push it all away, predicting for me futures I did not want to see.

Now nothing can change what is to come. A kingdom of pain will be mine, for I prayed for more rage and have been granted my wish.

My daughter is dead at my hand. Now wrath will be mine for all eternity. It was always in my nature. I am the killer, I am death—now too a monster made.

About the Author:

Zena Shapter writes from a castle in a flying city hidden by a thundercloud. Her writing reaches across ages and genre into the heart of storytelling. Author of 'Towards White' (IFWG 2017) and co-author of 'Into Tordon' (MidnightSun 2016 / Scholastic Distribution), she's won over a dozen national writing competitions – including a Ditmar Award, the Glen Miles Short Story Prize and the Australasian Horror Writers' Association Award for Short Fiction. Her short work has appeared in the Hugo-nominated 'Sci Phi Journal', 'Midnight Echo' (as well as their Australian Shadows Awarded 'best of' anthology), 'Antipodean SF' and Award-Winning Australian Writing (twice). Reviewer for Tangent Online Lillian Csernica has referred to her as a writer who "deserves your attention". She's a movie buff, keen traveller, story nerd, and inclusive creativity advocate, who's founded community creativity projects for writers such as the 'Art & Words Project' and the award-winning Northern Beaches Writers' Group. She's also a writing mentor, editor, book creator, HSC English tutor, Service NSW Creative Kids Provider, and short story judge. Find her online via every major social media platform and zenashapter.com

YOUR DEATH I DO FORTELL

Nikky Lee

"You'll die at the hands of an old woman," I tell him. Beside him, his fellow knights in arms snigger—until he flashes them a look that could silence the wind.

"How?"

I study the entrails: vines of gut, severed blossoms of kidney and liver. "You try to kill her," I say. "She defends herself. Better than you expect."

The knight's brows knit together beneath his mop of yellow curls. "An old woman?"

"Yes."

"Probably a Kultain spy," one lieutenant says, all squat and square-jawed. "Not to worry Captain, we'll route them out and put them to the noose."

My knight ignores him. Instead, he peers into the remains of the ram, face pale. No surprise, it's not every day you learn how you'll die.

He'd come in a swagger, expecting prophecy of fame and fortune, the ram he towed probably raided from a Kultain farm.

"When?" he asks.

I shrug. "That wasn't what you asked. Maybe tomorrow, maybe in a decade. Another question requires another offering." I motion to the ram strewn across the floor of my tent.

"You take us for easy marks, Witch?" The knight's second lieutenant growls, his glare near sharp enough to whet a knife on. He tosses down a bag of coin. "Take it and go. Don't be seen about camp or I'll string you up for the crows myself.

I scoop up the coins and bow, hiding my grin. "As it pleases you, sirs."

He finds me again on the dawn. Alone this time. Eyes puffy from lack of sleep as he presents me a rat, skinny as my little finger. "Another offering," he says.

"It won't yield much," I warn. And so it is when I crack open the rat's ribcage and splay its heart on the ground. "Soon." Is all I can tell him.

The knight considers the rat, eyes glazed as he sucks his lip. "Do you follow the gods?" he asks.

"I follow a god," I tell him. Somewhat true. "Not one from your pantheon."

"One of Kultain's—"

"An old god. You wouldn't know it."

"But an offering allows you to . . . see?"

"Aye, it does."

The knight stares at his hands, and I note how they quake. Slowly, he pulls off the pin of his Sun God from his breast. "What would it cost," he swallows, "to change my fate?"

I meet his gaze and pull on my power. "I suspect you know."

He sways. Then abruptly nods, stands and leaves my tent. Minutes later, the screaming starts. I arrange myself behind my curtains and wait.

The knight returns, the heads of his two lieutenants under each arm. "Is it enough?" he asks, breathless. "There are more outside." When I check, bodies line the path to my tent like paving stones.

"Very well." I turn. "I accept your offering." My fortune teller visage cracks, glamour sloughing away. My back hunches, the ragged bones of someone's grandmother turning me old and withered. My hair flows grey. Wrinkles score my skin. A pair of ram's horns curl from my temples; a rat's tail twitches at my feet. But the mark of these offerings will soon fade and I will have a new form; with so many sacrifices to choose from.

The knight blinks, my spell over him unravelling. He screams, draws his blade, and swings. I flex my magic, drawing on his last offering. It begins at my hands, my hag fingers lose their wrinkles, my grip turns young and powerful. With god-like speed I duck and my sink my knife through his heart. He gargles.

"But . . . you accepted . . ."

"You're right, I did." With a twist, my face morphs to match his subordinate's—the lieutenant with the sharp glare. A fine offering indeed. The last of the transformation ripples over me. I flex my new shoulders, roll my supple neck. A crone no more. "I trust this shall suffice?"

About the Author:

Nikky grew up as a barefoot 90s child in Perth, Western Australia, before moving to New Zealand in 2016. By day she works as a professional content writer and by night authors speculative fiction, often burning the candle at both ends to explore fantastic worlds, mine asteroids and meet wizards. Her creative work has appeared in magazines, on radio and in anthologies around the world. She is currently writing a dark fantasy trilogy, routinely sacrificing literary darlings to the editing gods in the hopes of seeing it published.

You can find her online at:
W:nikkythewriter.com | T:@NikkyMLee | F:nikkythewriter

Night Train to Colchis

BG Hilton

The station at Olympos was new, as were all the stations back then. Black soot had not yet stained the white marble. The building stood, ghostlike, in the middle of the night. Empty, save for a lone ticket seller. A limestone road, silver in the moonlight, ran past the station before disappearing into the east and west. Two deep, parallel grooves lay in the road, paths for the bronze wheels of the *diolkos* train. Twenty or thirty of us piled into this empty station, killing the silence dead with our banter. While Jason argued with the ticket seller, I cast my eyes up at Olympos—the great mountain home of the gods—towering over us, huge and eerie. Perhaps the sight of the home of the gods should have given us pause, but it didn't. We were all far, far too drunk to worry what gods might want.

Start from the beginning, eh? Our little gang were rich kids, mostly. Nobles, minor royalty and—just to prove we weren't snobs— the occasional scion of a wealthy merchant. We were old enough to have crawled out from under the thumbs of our tutors, but not so old our fathers twisted our arms to do something useful. We were at Olympos for the Holy Games. None of us were competing that year, so after the opening ceremony we hauled a cartload of wine around to Caenus' place and had a bit of an old symposium. Crack some amphorae, have the slaves put out some olives, some barbequed octopus—a nice night, yeah?

But you know how it is—you get a good symposium going, everyone is all mellow, and then some jackass pulls out a lyre and starts strumming away. This time it was Orpheus, and say what you will, the lad's got a decent voice. Everyone asked him to play something we could sing along to but Orpheus—being Orpheus—started singing a twenty-minute ode about a magical sheep.

How did it go? Poseidon, in the form of a ram, impregnated a nymph who was in the form of a ewe? As you do. And their son was a golden ram with wings or something, and a bunch of people with hard-to-remember names escaped from someplace I've never heard of to another place that I forget. Anyway, the winged ram died and became the constellation of Aries, while its fleece ended up in a tree guarded by a dragon and a bunch of magic bulls—which frankly sounded like a bunch of magic bull to me.

"Sheriously," I said. "I mean seriously. Think about it: what happened to the sheep's *wings*? How did they manage to get its fleece off with the wings in the way? Eh? Doesn't make sense."

"Mutton wings," Hercules said. He was already about three amphorae in, and moving from happy-drunk to hungry-drunk. We were hoping he'd go from there to pass-out-drunk, because it was *never* fun when Hercules got *angry*-drunk.

"Mutton wings, fricasseed in a nice olive oil and slathered with hot sauce," he added. "Tasty. Where did you say this sheep is, Orph?"

"The Fleece resides in Colchis," Orpheus said. "Perhaps its wings are there, too."

"Well let's go to Colchis," Hercules said, leaning on his club as he stood. "Bring a pan."

"There won't be any meat left on the wings," Laertes called out. "That's what Nestor was saying, wasn't it?"

"No," I began, "I said there aren't any—"

"I don't think you follow," Orpheus interrupted, with a sneer. "Firstly, Colchis is a very long way away—on the far side of the Black Sea, in fact. Secondly, the Fleece is not a physical object, it is a metaphor, a symbolic representation of—"

"Where's! My! Bloody! Mutton! Wings!" Hercules bellowed, smashing his club against Caenus' mosaic floor with every syllable. "I'm! Bloody! Hungry!"

It was looking grim. We were already well drunk and it seemed we were going to have concussions on top of hangovers the next day. We were probably going to end up missing tomorrow's nude, oiled-up men's wrestling—and I *liked* the oiled-up nude wrestling. Hell, we *all* liked the oiled-up nude wrestling. Bloody Hercules was always ruining things like that.

And then Jason stuck his nose in.

"Colchis?" he said, in that annoying little voice of his. "I can get us to Colchis."

The poets will tell you Jason was a missing prince raised by a centaur, true king of Iolcos, blah, blah, blah. Truth was, he was a lesser Thessalian royal and his family gave him a generous allowance just to stay the Hades away from Thessaly. He travelled around here and there, couch surfing mostly. People tolerated him because he was as generous as he was rich, but he was *so annoying*. He would get completely fascinated by some tedious thing and then wouldn't shut up about it—until he found the next thing to get excited about and then the cycle would begin anew.

"Colchis," he repeated. "Getting there's as easy as pi, and far more rational, hyeah! We just take the *diolkos*."

"Shut up," I whispered.

Castor—or maybe Pollux—said: "Is this about ships again, Jase? Because honestly, if I hear another story about that trireme of yours . . ."

"Triremes?" Jason laughed. "Things of the past. I don't even have the *Argo* any more. Sold it to a man in Corinth—a very *backwards* man in Corinth, if I may say so, hyeah! Yesterday's news, *triremes*!"

"Shut up," I said, a little louder.

"Why, from here at Olympos, we simply take the midnight *diolkos* to Hellespont," Jason said. "At dawn, we take a boat across to Troy. From there we transfer to the Lydia and West Persia Road-Groove Network."

"For Zeus' sake, shut up," I said.

"We travel on to Sinope," Jason continued, "transfer to the Black Sea and Caucasus Line to Colchis. They've got broad-gauge road-grooves there, so that should be *very* interesting. The whole trip can't take us much longer than a week. Probably. I mean, they are doing some signal repairs between Sisamos and Ionopolis due to Harpy damage, but if we were to take the local service instead of the express . . ."

To my surprise, Jason had helped after all. Hercules wasn't angry any more. His eyelids were drooping and he looked like he was dozing on his feet.

"I don't know about them *diolk*-things." He yawned. "Jus' wan' some tasty sheep wings. Don't trust those bloody engines . . ."

"Hah!" said Pollux. Or maybe it was Castor. "The great Hercules, afraid of a moving box!"

Well that did it. Hercules eyes were wide open and his face was flushed again. "Afraid am I?" he bellowed. "We'll see about that. I'm going on the *diolkos*, and so's everyone else! We're all going to Colchis, no exceptions. Jason, tickets are on you."

"Right-o!" Jason beamed.

Was it a good idea? Well, it was better than a beating.

And that's how we came to be at the Olympos Station, blind drunk but still carrying as many amphorae as we could. This is before they banned wine on the *diolkos* routes—a decision that followed suspiciously soon after our journey.

We chatted and drank in the warm summer air until the *diolkos* arrived. I'd never ridden one before, but of course I'd seen them about. They were building the bloody things from Sparta to Macedonia, from Delphi to Persepolis. The first carriage was always issuing smoke, and this one was no exception. Thick clouds plumed from its windows, and the fires within were visible in the dim light.

In painful detail, Jason explained how it all worked. A brass globe full of water is heated, sending steam through bent tubes. This causes the globe to spin, and a system of gears transferred that power to the wheels. The system was controlled by some sort of device that they make on Antikythera . . . I lost interest after that. Well, realistically I lost interest before that, but at least I was still listening.

The train of carriages shuddered to a halt. By an unfortunate turn of fate, I was closest to a door. I hesitated just long enough for Hercules to shove me out of the way.

"Move it, dweeb," he said, hauling himself on board.

Reluctantly, I followed him. Inside, the carriage was a largely featureless box, with a few holes pierced in the side to let the air in. Rough wooden chairs were nailed to the floor, and I was just tired enough for them to look comfortable. The ceiling had once been decorated with a scene of satyrs and centaurs frolicking in Arcadia, but even though it was fairly new much of it had come away in flakes.

"The vibrations," Jason sighed. "Murder on the frescoes."

"Well why paint them then?" Pollux asked.

Jason frowned. "Well you have to paint frescoes. That's just common sense."

We were all still pretty drunk. When the *diolkos* began moving it was a little nauseating and Caenus was sick out of one of the wall holes. But after a while, we grew used to the gentle motion of the machine, which lulled us to sleep.

Dawn was rising over Hellespont when we awoke. The sun reflected off the water and shone through the hole in the wall, right into my face. The others blearily came to, and discussions on what a bad idea this had been started. But there were hot food stalls at Hellespont Station and we were too hungry not to get off and eat.

"Let's go back," said Castor and Pollux together.

"Whose idea was this?" Hercules demanded, as he tucked into his third plate of dolmades.

"You mean we aren't going all the way to Colchis?" Jason asked. He looked like his feelings hadn't just been hurt but brutally beaten and thrown in a dungeon on bread and water.

"I say we push on," Orpheus sighed. "Hear me out: it's all about the story. We go back now, we have to tell everyone what really happened, yeah? Then we're nothing but a bunch of drunken yobs. But if we press on, we go see this Fleece thing—we come back heroes."

"But the nude wrestling . . ." I said.

"Do you want to be a laughing stock, Nestor?" Orpheus said. "Because I don't. I worked hard for my reputation as the coolest guy in Greece, and I'm not going back and admitting that I went on a drunken sheep-wing run, for Zeus' sake!"

The rest of us looked . . . well, well we looked sheepish, I guess. No one said anything, but we all knew what we had to do. When you're young, drunk and stupid you don't *stop* in the middle of something idiotic—you *press on* damn it. So when our stomachs settled, we got on the boat, covered our ears against the drum and creak of oars, and crossed to Asia. I ended up sitting next to Jason. Of course. And yes, he spent the crossing talking about which oil lamps work best in signal boxes.

At the Asian shore, we trudged over to the station that they'd built near the ruins of Troy. An enterprising Lydian had set up a small wooden horse and for half a drachma he'd sketch you riding it. Hercules was the only taker, but I had to admit that the Lydian sketched a fair likeness.

The *diolkos* was delayed and while we waited, Castor and Pollux disappeared for a while. They turned up just in time wearing identical smug expressions and claiming to have gotten lucky with a hen's party from Lemnos. When the *diolkos* did arrive, it was newer than the first one. It had slightly bigger holes in the walls, making it much easier to watch the countryside go past. And I didn't have to sit next to Jason.

We picked up wine at each stop and passed the journey drinking, singing, and telling rude stories. When the mood took us, we'd draw penises on the seats. It was actually kind of fun. Granted, one time we accidentally killed King Cyzicus when he walked into the wrong carriage and had to pay for his burial. In Sinope, the train was delayed by cliffs that repeatedly crashed together.

But mostly the journey was pleasant.

It took about a week to get to Colchis. Turns out that while Orpheus thought Colchis was a town, it was actually a whole country. When we finished mocking Orph, we asked around to find out where the Fleece was. Most of the locals spoke a weird dialect, but I find if you speak Greek very loudly and clearly, anyone can get the gist of it. Even so, it was Jason who figured it out in the end. He spoke to the *diolkos* people in some secret nerd language of nasal vowels and pop-culture references.

"The Fleece is not hard to find," he said. "It's near a small station on the north-eastern branch line. The locals are actually pretty keen on people coming to have a look, hyeah!"

The *diolkos* that took us there was a small, dingy local line. Instead of spreading out like usual, we had to squeeze together to accommodate blank-eyed locals carrying heavy baskets and live chickens. Eventually, we reached the correct station and started asking around for the Fleece. It didn't take long for a man to appear at the station, smiling and shaking everyone's hand.

He was tall, clearly of Greek descent but dressed in the manner of the Scythians. Not showing any leg, you know the sort of thing. Socks with sandals. Ugh.

"Ah hello, is it not?" he said in broken Greek. "How are you, maybe? Welcome to Areopolis, home of Fleece of golden, yes."

"Greetings!" Orpheus intoned. "We are weary travellers from Greece."

"Yes, so I see, my friendly," the man said. "I am Aëetes, head of local tourist-man office. You are here for see Fleece, maybe?"

"I guess so." Jason shrugged. Now that the *diolkos* journey had come to an end, he had lost interest in the whole exercise.

"You are in luck, old chums!" Aëetes said. "Fleece that is golden is attraction of town. Many tourist-men come to see. You need guidebook? Only twenty drachmas, bargain!"

"We don't need a guidebook, we need to see the Fleece," Castor said.

"See it?" Pollux said. "I thought we were bringing it back home?"

"And there was something about food, wasn't there?" Hercules said, scratching his beard. "I'm pretty sure there was some mention of wings."

Aëetes smiled broadly. "You want see Fleece? Is thirty drachmas per head, cheap. But if you want *take* Fleece, different. Must face challenges. Most deadly tests of courage and strength, yes—and comes at cost of one thousand drachmas! Also twenty drachmas per person for everyone who wants to watch. No, I like you boys—I make fifteen drachma, because is good deal, maybe? My daughter come, sell you tickets. Medea? Medea?"

Jason grimaced and looked back towards the station. "I don't know. We came here, hyeah? Can't we just pretend we saw the Fleece and go . . ."

Then Medea turned up, and Jason couldn't finish his sentence. Not with his mouth hanging open like that. I thought she was pretty okay looking—you know, for a woman. To Jason she was clearly Aphrodite and Helen of Troy rolled into one.

"You boys going to try to win the Golden Fleece?" She spoke much better Greek than her father, and spoke it in a low, sultry voice. "Many have tried . . . will *you* be the ones to succeed?"

There was a moment's uncertainty. It ended when she arched an eyebrow at Jason and the little fellow went bright red and almost choked. Hercules pounded him on the back, which really wasn't very helpful.

"I will win the Fleece!" Jason declared, once he'd picked himself off the ground. "I will slay that dragon!"

"You could bore it to death by talking about *diolkos* timetables," I said.

"You are *so* brave!" Medea said. Jason preened while the rest of us rolled our eyes.

Jason's purse was nearly empty, so we had a whip around for cash for tickets. Once we'd paid, Medea and her father led us out of town to a small paddock where some mangy cattle slept. At the centre of this paddock was a dead tree. Over one branch hung a long, floppy tube that might have been a dragon, or else a very large sock. On another branch hung . . . something. Something that glinted like metal in the sunlight.

"Not a real object?" Hercules said. "A metaphor for prosperity?"

"Just because it's a metaphor doesn't mean it's not real too," Orpheus said.

"But you said . . ."

"You know nothing of poetry."

Aëetes pointed to the cattle. "First task of winning Fleece, you must yolk fire-breathing bulls. Then, field is ploughed with them, maybe?"

I peered over the fence to get a closer look at the nearest bull—a scrawny, fly-blown looking thing that chewed its cud with a world-weary expression.

"Mate, these bulls wouldn't breath fire if you poured hot sauce down their gullets," I said.

"Stand back! I will yolk these terrible creatures!" Jason said. "I'm quite good at yolks. Did you know that the standard Greco-Thracian yolk has only been in use for the last fifty years? But you're probably using a Colcian style yolk, which has some advantages in terms of mechanical . . ."

Medea pouted very slightly and Jason fell silent. I must say, I was warming to the girl.

Anyway, long story short, Jason went to yolk the bulls. His detailed theoretical knowledge of ploughing didn't help him much, even with such docile creatures. It was nearing nightfall when he pointed to a field that was criss-crossed by ragged zig-zaggy furrows and could—by a very generous assessment—be considered 'ploughed'.

"Behold, Aëetes," he proclaimed, "the first task is complete."

Aëetes looked up from the scroll that he'd been reading for the last four hours. "Yes, yes, much good." He yawned. "Very hero, unquestioned. Now you must fight undead warriors. My friend, you plant teeth of dragon in field, and then . . . how do you say it in Greek? Ah, you grow many boners, yes?"

"*What?*"

"And then you must *spank* boners!"

"The teeth grow into *skeletons*, Papa," Medea sighed. "Not boners. Jason must *fight* the skeletons."

"Yes, it is so, maybe."

"Also, Papa, we have no more dragon teeth," Medea said. "Remember when we ran out of decorations for your spooky costume party and you said to use the teeth . . ."

"Oh, yes, I remember," Aëetes sighed. "Second round, victory by default to Mr Jaxon. Now for thirdly, final and lastly, you fight dragon!"

In the dying light, we all marched up to the tree. "If this is anything like those other tasks, it shouldn't take long," Caenus said.

"Ten drachma say that the dragon's a serious threat," Orpheus said.

"You're on!"

Jason drew his sword and approached the 'dragon'. Up close, it looked even more like a long sock than it had from a distance. Then its head moved—and I saw that it was actually a huge serpent with vestigial legs and wings. It hissed—revealing a mouth completely empty of teeth.

A ripple of laughter ran through our midst.

"Piece of cake!" Jason said, raising his blade.

"That's ten drachmas you owe me!" Caenus smiled at Orpheus.

As if on signal, the dragon hurled itself from its branch and onto the shrieking Jason. His sword fell to the ground as the creature curled itself around him, squeezing with all its might. He tried to wrestle with the creature, but it just squeezed tighter.

"I'm not okay," Jason wheezed. "Aaah! Crapping pantsbuckets, it . . . Ow! My ribs!"

"Called it!" Orpheus smirked. "Rule of Three. Literary theory saves the day again. Pay up, Caenus."

We watched as Jason slowly stopped thrashing, not quite certain what to do. Finally Hercules sighed, shouldered his way through the crowd and held out his hand to the struggling Jason.

"Tag me," he said.

Jason tagged him. I thought Hercules was going to do something clever, but he just grabbed the dragon by the throat and punched it in the face until it released Jason. It slithered back up its tree and looked down, sulkily.

"Victory!" Jason croaked. "I have won the Fleece! Be a friend, Hercules, and pass it down to me."

As Medea helped Jason to his feet, the rest of us examined the Fleece in the dying light. Honestly, I half expected it to be a goat-pelt painted yellow, but it looked like what would happen if you let King Midas in a petting zoo. I peered closer, examining every tiny, wavy filament of gold thread that extended from the sheepskin backing. There were even a couple of holes in the shoulder where a pair of wings might once have extended.

"It's real," I said. "I'd stake my life on it."

"Real, sure, you win real Fleece," Aëetes said, sadly. "Big heroes. Too bad, is town's attraction to tourist-men. Much sad, but you win, square and fair. I wrap it up for you, maybe?"

In hindsight, we should have noticed how keen Aëetes was to get us back onto the *diolkos*. For someone who wanted us to spend all our money, you'd think he'd try to talk us into taking rooms for the night, right? Or try some scam to win back the Fleece? But it had been a long day after a longer trip and we weren't particularly observant.

The *diolkos* journey home was more awkward than the run to Colchis. Jason had lost all interest in timetables, so we made some pretty bad mistakes. We ran into some sirens, though fortunately we had Orpheus' singing to drown them out. Orph was pretty insufferable after that, but I guess that was marginally better than being lured to our deaths. And apparently we got in fight with a big brass robot—but I slept through that one, so it could be the others were talking crap.

In spite of these unwanted side trips, the rumbling, hissing engines bore us home on wheels of bronze. One by one the gang were dropped off at their respective stations until it was just Jason, Orpheus and me, tired, bored, lounging in our seats and listening to the gentle clicking of the wheels.

"Well, your family will be happy," I said to Jason. "They said you'd never amount to much, and here you are with the Golden Fleece."

"Yes, it's pretty nice . . ." Jason sighed.

"You're still thinking about Medea, aren't you?" Orpheus said.

"Maybe I should go back for her," Jason said.

"Dude, *never* go back for a girl," Orpheus said. "Makes you look desperate. You won't catch *me* doing something like that."

I was half-listening, staring at the parcel that Aëetes had wrapped. In the days since we'd left Colchis, I'd been thinking about it a lot. Sure he'd wrapped the parcel right in front of us, but we hadn't been paying a lot of attention, you know? We'd been cheering, patting Hercules on the back, toasting our success with overpriced Colchian wine and trying to resuscitate Jason.

"Jason," I said. "Maybe you should open that package."

"What, on the *diolkos*?" he said. "Someone might see the gold. It's not safe."

"Indulge me."

The only other passengers in the carriage were a couple of elderly philosophers from Sardis who were napping in a corner. Even so, Jason angled his body to block any possible sight they might have of his treasure as he untied the string and peeled back a corner of the linen to reveal . . .

"A goat pelt, painted yellow!" Jason gasped.

"We've been Fleeced!" Orpheus cried.

Jason and I both glared at him. He shrugged. "I sussed to Aëetes' game ages ago. Been sitting on that joke for *days*."

So, that's the real story of the Argonauts. Even if he was a prick, Orpheus did his job and sang songs of our journey that made everyone think we were big heroes instead of drunken yahoos. We all went back to our normal lives, other than the occasional humble-brag when someone mentioned the Fleece.

Jason was the exception. He went back to Colchis. He said he was going to get the real Fleece from Aëetes, but we all knew he was going after Medea. Last we heard, they'd married. I just hope Jason didn't lose interest in *her*. She didn't seem like the type who'd take it well.

About the Author:

BG Hilton studied English at the University of Sydney; Writing at UTS, and writes when he's not wrangling his baby. He blogs about Frankenstein movies, the Leonard Nimoy TV series In Search Of . . . (aka Great Mysteries of the World) and also writes a free series of rambling soap-operatic spec-fic web stories at bghilton.com. You can also find him on Twitter @bghilton.

His short stories have been published in several venues, including Andromeda Spaceways, Antipodean SF and an upcoming story on Pseudopod. His first novel, a steampunk adventure story will be coming out from Odyssey Books in the near future. He lives in Sydney, but don't hold that against him.

Aries Witches

Lisa Rodrigues

I was born unto the Aries sign
In my world that meant God cursed me
My parents did their duty still
Lest they face the witch's mercy

I knew that when I turned sixteen
I would be left to wander
Alone into the blackest wood
And find my calling with her

With nightmares of a ragged hag
The village children mocked me
But I steeled my heart and made my plans
From their taunts, I'd soon be free

LISA RODRIGUES

I let them pack me with supplies
And sneer to see me go
Watched by the gnarled trees overhead
And the mossy earth below

I planned to disappear that day
Leave the witch's curse behind me
But the woods beyond the twisting path
Were far too thick and wildly

As darkness fell the cold crept in
And I hastened in my step
It was then the path began to glow
And my will to fight did ebb

My step was dragged and my heartbeat low
As I came upon the cabin
I barely marked the cheery front
The cold had left me ashen

I fell upon the doorstep
And thumped upon the door
My heart raced from the fear of it
But I feared the cold much more

ARIES WITCHES

A beauty I did not expect
To greet me with her mercy
She set me 'fore a raging fire
And asked me of my journey

We shared our tales of woe that night
We shared our lives, our sins
She too was marked under the ram
And turned out by her kin

She came upon this cottage
Crumbling and overgrown
She fixed it, held the woods at bay
And now she called it home

It was she who claimed of witchcraft
To keep the world of man at bay
To stave off abuse or murder
As in her time was the way

She sprinkled the first rumours
And planted shrooms to light the way
Aries girls were no longer harmed
No longer the world's prey

At sixteen they were sent to her

And had the choice to stay

The other girls like me had gone

To discover their own way

The fire lit her golden hair

And the sadness in her eyes

My stomach fluttered when she moved

To sit close by my side

A warmth began inside me

A rare spell had been cast

I held her hand and met her eyes

And knew I was home at last

About the Author:

Lisa Rodrigues is a Eurasian Australian writer in her 30-somethings living in Perth. She writes poetry and has written speculative fiction on and off for years. She works fulltime in tourism marketing, and when she's not working or writing she can be found doing acrobatics or cheerleading.

She has been previously published in braind.rip magazine and is currently working on short stories and flash fiction. You can find more of her work at endofnext.wordpress.com.

RAM'S REVENGE

Nikky Lee

I never meant to kill Sir Woolston. I mean, the ram was a prick and an arse, but I didn't really mean him dead. At least, not dead under a truck. Dad kept him in the front paddock, where he couldn't ram the rest of the flock. And every day Sir Woolston would chase me through the grass, wicked horns bent low, aimed at my backside as I sprinted to the bus stop. Every day since middle school; since Dad sat me down three years ago and said:

"Emma, you'll need to take the bus from now on, okay?"

Mum had just passed and between taking care of Nan and keeping the farm afloat, he couldn't spare the hour-long drive to school anymore. I'd given him a mute nod, privately relieved. That hour had been Mum's and mine. Doing the drive with Dad wouldn't have been the same. So, at the age of thirteen, I packed my bag of books, a soggy sandwich, and ran for the door.

For as long as I can remember, I've always been late. Time passes differently for me; one moment I have thirty minutes until the bus comes, the next I spot it trundling up the road from the kitchen window. Like I did that first morning. Taking a shortcut across Sir Woolston's paddock seemed harmless enough that first time. What could one old ram past his prime do anyway?

I arrived at school with my butt bruised purple and ram-shaped teeth marks all down one forearm.

So began Sir Woolston's and my long-standing vendetta.

People say sheep are stupid. I tell them they haven't met Sir Woolston. I mean, that ram was as devious as he was vicious. Sometimes, he'd let me get within cooee of the paddock's front gate—right where the bus would stop—before springing out from behind the old gum to run me down. He'd herd me into potholes so I'd trip until I had every hidden drop and rise in that entire field memorised better than the alphabet.

The day he died began like any other. I was running late, as always. A glint of bus through the gums lining the road and I surged to my feet, snatching my bag up, pecking a kiss on Nan asleep in her recliner, and bolting through the door, fly screen snapping shut at my heels.

He was waiting for me, that prig of a sheep, as always. His beady little eyes trained on my approach. *Spiteful bastard,* I thought, pulling the straps of my backpack tight as I hurried to the rusty barbed wire fence. I gingerly pushed my homemade step up against one post. I'd made it one weekend, not long after that first scuffle with Sir Woolston; it had served me well in the three years since. Step secured, I climbed up it and onto the top of the post. It wobbled under me, as always, and I balanced on it, poised like a diver about to take the plunge.

Sir Woolston let out a low rumbling bleat and backed up two steps. Then he lowered his head.

"Come at me," I snarled. Down the road, the bus revved closer. One hundred meters away, max. Miss it and it'd be an hour before another came, and more to the point, I'd be sentenced to scratching gum off the underside of school desks. Mr Lombard had made me that promise last week.

I sucked in a breath, tensed my muscles, and sprang. My feet hit the grass and I bolted, arms pumping. *Go. Go, go, go.* Behind, Sir Woolston bellowed and launched towards me. I jumped Pythagoras' pothole, sidestepped Gauss' hidden log (yes, I named all the obstacles after mathematicians, for all the hell they'd put me through). With a "ha" I cleared Leibniz's rock, almost invisible in the long grass. Sir Woolston closed in. That was always the way of it. Four legs are quicker than two. His hooves thundered at my back, so close I could hear him snorting through his nose. My only chance came down to timing.

I twisted a glance over my shoulder. And there he was, right behind me. Angry little eyes burning holes into the butt of my jeans. He lowered his head and sprang. I threw myself sideways, a 90-degree change of direction. Sir Woolston shot past, one horn nearly catching my shirt.

"Thought you had me, didn't you?" I gasped out, clutching a stitch in my side. Sir Woolston slowed and turned, malleable lips twitching to show his flat teeth. *Just piss off,* I willed at him. Not to be.

The stubborn bastard came on again. I turned and ran, bag bouncing on my back. Ahead, the bus pulled up to my stop—

—My foot squelched into a pile of sheep shit. Only, it had rained last night, so instead of the usual dry pellets, this was a sodden, soggy mass. My foot skidded out from under me. My world teetered. Arms windmilled.

Wham!

I hit the ground. Pain shot across my backside, up my back. Sir Woolston was on me in a heartbeat, fierce little teeth sinking into my arm as I tried to batter him away.

"Get off you prick!" I staggered to my feet.

Wham!

Fresh pain radiated down my left quadriceps. My leg went dead, nearly buckling under my weight. Bloody corked my thigh, he did. Fucking ram. I slipped my bag off one shoulder, covered in mud and shit, and swung it at Sir Woolston's head. Eight kilos of book and soggy sandwich collected him with a satisfying thunk. *Take that, bastard.* He swayed, black eyes momentarily dazed. Or perhaps surprised. I didn't stick around to find out which it was. I skedaddled, hightailing it for the bus. Through the doors, the driver checked his watch.

Don't you leave. Don't you dare fucking leave. I lengthened my stride. Somewhere behind, Sir Woolston let out another of those rumbling bleats. Stubborn git. I reached the gate, stuck one toe then another between the wooden slats and climbed.

Wham!

Sir Woolston barrelled into the gate. There was a crack of splintering wood and the gate buckled under me. My grip slipped, and I pitched headfirst over the railing, felt something—an exposed nail or bit of splintered wood perhaps—catch my jeans. With an awful, slow ripping sound my descent slowed and plonked me, headfirst, onto the road.

I scrambled up, saw the tear. It began just above my knee and went all the way to the ankle. A dribble of blood stained the edge. I ran a finger along the rip; the edges were already fraying. A fist closed inside my throat.

They weren't just any old jeans. These were mum's jeans. A bit baggy, sure, and *technically* I wasn't supposed to wear them at school, with them not meeting the school's fluid understanding of uniform and all, but I hadn't cared. They smelled like her. Eucalyptus and lemon. Even after all my washing them.

My vision grew hot. Then red.

"Bloody ram!" I screamed. My foot lashed out, striking the gate. The wood was harder than I'd expected, and pain shot through my toes.

Sir Woolston just stared. Black eyes unblinking. Rage boiled inside me. I wanted to wrap my hands around that bloody ram's throat and squeeze; get Dad's shotgun from the ute and fire it between his Goddamn eyeballs.

"Piece of shit! Go die already!" I kicked again, this time connecting with one of the rusty hinges. There was a ping of metal snapping. The gate gave under my sneaker. With a creak, then a groan, the whole thing toppled over.

I was too angry to care. I glared at the ram through the broken gate, thinking murder until a blast from the bus horn made me jump. Sir Woolston skittered back. *Yea, you better run.*

"Are you getting on or not?" The driver shouted through the doors. "I've not got all day."

I didn't recognise him. A newbie then. Probably the first time he'd seen my daily rush across the paddock. I nodded, gathered my bag and stalked to my seat.

As the bus pulled away, I glanced out the dust-covered window. Sir Woolston had picked his way out through the wreckage of the gate and was standing on the road, watching my bus retreat into the distance.

"I hope you get hit by a car," I raged under my breath, inspecting the rip in my jeans again.

As it turned out, fate did one better. That afternoon, I later learned, Sir Woolston met his end under the wheel of a thirty-tonne cattle truck.

It was dusk when I returned home and made my long, slow walk up our winding drive. Gravel slid and ground under my shoes, the staples I'd used to hold the tear shut in my—*mum's*—jeans chafed a rash into my leg. When the road eventually rounded alongside Sir Woolston's paddock, I made to glare at the beastly ram inside, only to find it empty.

Weird. But not unheard of. Dad must have moved him into another paddock, what with the gate broke and all. A flicker of guilt rose in me at that. I could have texted him about it, but I'd been so angry the thought hadn't occurred to me.

I clomped up the steps of our two-storey farmhouse, along our paint-peeled veranda, and stopped, hand hovering over the knob of the flyscreen as I heard the voices in the living room. Strange voices.

"We could start the listing at one point five, but I can't promise you'll get that," a husky baritone was saying, as if it had spent its life on the end of a cigarette.

"There isn't any way to bump it up?" Dad's voice. My stomach clenched. His words had that distinct waver he got when he was nervous, or anxious—or sad. I'd heard it down the end of the phone line and I'd never forget it. *Emma, it's Mum.*

"I can paint the house—" Dad said.

A sigh. "It needs more than a fresh lick of paint, Reece. Your barn's infested with termites, the fences are rusting, gates are broken, your tractor doesn't look like it's been used in years."

They were right about the tractor, whomever it was. About all of it, come to think of it.

"The state things are in here," it continued. "You'll be lucky to get any offers over one mil."

Understanding dawned. My jaw dropped. *He wouldn't!* I yanked the screen open, shoved open the door—unlocked as always—and stormed in.

"You can't sell the farm!" It came out louder than intended and so close to hysteria I winced. Damn voice, betraying me at a time like this. I swallowed, took a breath, and turned on Dad perched on the arm of the couch. "You can't really be thinking—?"

"Ah, Emma, you're home early." Dad looked guilty, like the time I'd caught him with a hand inside my spare change jar.

Beside him, a man with greying hair and equally grey suit stood up. "Let's call it a day." He shuffled the pile of papers and real estate brochures together. I recognised the logo for one of the nursing home's in the city on one of them.

"We're not selling," I told him.

Dad stood up, wringing his hands. "Emma—"

"No!" I said. I didn't want to hear it. Excuses. That's all it would be.

"It's Nan, Emma," he went on, ignoring me. "She's getting worse." His gaze flicked to Nan asleep in her recliner, eyes roaming under her eyelids. "She called me Michael this morning." Dad's brother, dead some ten years now. Cancer. I don't remember him well.

"She was just confused," I said.

The real estate agent gave a little cough, picked up his briefcase and with a nod to Dad, slid out the door. I don't think Dad even noticed. Instead, he rubbed his face, as if trying to scrub off the guilt. He sighed.

"She's been confused for a while now. Haven't you noticed?"

I stood seething before the couch and my father slumped further into it. I didn't answer. Truth was, I had noticed. Nan had always been a bit eccentric, to my mind. She used to make all her own clothes—and many of mine as a kid—crocheting sweaters and blankets in the brightest, most clashing colours she could find. For as long as I could remember, she'd never worn a matching pair of socks.

But recently, the sharp wit under those short, grey curls, had grown blunt. She slept more. Forgot what pills she'd taken at breakfast. Put yogurt in her tea instead of milk. There was a time when I opened the freezer and found her dentures in it. My chest squeezed at the memory, like I was being smothered in a too-tight hug. Of course I'd noticed Nan slipping away. Of course I *knew*. But neither one of us had said it. Saying it out loud made it real. I swallowed. This day was really going to the dumps.

"I worry about leaving her on her own for so long," Dad went on. "She needs a carer."

"Then I will come home early from school. Stay with her on weekends," I said, desperate.

Dad shook his head. He reached out, took my hands in his and gave them a squeeze. "Emma, it's not enough. And I can't ask you to do that." He looked past me, to Nan, and his expression softened to the point where I wondered if he might cry. With a swallow he returned to me. "With the sale of the farm we could put her in a care home, somewhere nice. And we could get an apartment close by."

I pulled my hands free. "An *apartment*?" The thought of being crammed into a fifty by square metre shoebox made my insides curl.

Dad was quiet a moment, then his gaze drifted to Nan again. "It probably won't be for long."

My chest tightened. This was Nan we were talking about. Her marbles might have a few pebbles and bits of twine in the bag, but she wasn't like she'd sent them scattering across the floor. She was still there. Albeit intermittently.

Dad stood and ran his fingers through his hair. "I wish there was another way, Em. I really do. But I can't see it."

I stared up at him, the lump from this morning clogging my throat again. "But what about Mum?" My mind flittered along the track we'd worn up the hill out back, stopping at the old Karri tree there, the one

Mum used to read under in the summer, and the tombstone next to it.

Dad wouldn't meet my eyes, but I saw the water in his, and suddenly I was struck by how tired he looked. Like he'd spent sleepless nights making this decision. So, I knew his answer long before he spoke. "I'm sorry."

Something inside my chest cracked, probably a rib as he cut out my heart and strangled it. Heat crept up my throat, behind my nose. I clenched my jaw to stop my chin wobbling and strode for the door, banging it shut behind me.

Across the veranda. *Breathe.* Down the steps—skip the middle one that creaks. *Walk. Breathe and walk.* Crunch along the driveway.

And that's when I saw him on the back of Dad's ute. The tarp Dad had used to keep the flies off had blown loose, revealing a lolling blue tongue, bloody wool and a broken horn. One dry, elongated pupil stared out at me, accusing. Sir Woolston. Dead as fucking dead.

Dad loved Sir Woolston. God knew why, the ram was as much of a prick to him as it was to me. Sir Woolston had been a gift from Mum's dad when they'd married and he'd handed over the reins of the farm to them.

We buried Sir Woolston in his paddock. Out under the big gum. Well, Dad did. I watched from the veranda, dazed and adrift, not sure what to feel. Banjo, our ginger tom, rubbed his face against my shoulder, tail curling under my chin as I slouched on the top step.

The farm, Dad was selling the farm. The thought spin-cycled through my head. Round and round.

A clunk of a shovel dropped on the gravel drive signalled Dad's return. He slumped down next to me, peeling off his gardening gloves. Bits of wool and blood stuck to them. His cheeks were flushed and sweat clung to the collar of his shirt.

"He had a good run, Sir Woolston did. I'm sad to see him go."

I wasn't. And I wouldn't have minded if Sir Woolston's run had been a good deal shorter, but saying that would only upset Dad, so I nodded. A silence stalked over us. I let it settle and dig in its claws, and Dad shifted, uncomfortable, until at last, he turned to me. I kept my gaze on the paddock, though out of the corner of my eye, there was that wrinkle in his brow when he knew he'd done wrong.

"I'm sorry, Emma. I should have told you sooner. But it's the only way."

No, it's the easy way, I thought, and very nearly said. But I didn't. Words are like barbed wire. You want to pick through them carefully or else the barbs sink in. And if you're not careful about it, the wounds will go bad and fester. Mum had taught me that. I picked at the tear in my jeans and, because Banjo was nudging, scratched under the tom's chin.

"What about the animals?" I heard myself say.

Dad shifted again. "Well if the new owners want to keep them, we'll include them in the sale."

"And if they don't?"

"We'll find homes for some, sell off the others."

"And if we can't sell them?"

There was the slightest pause from him, then, "they'll go to the abattoir."

My lips pressed tight. It wasn't like we hadn't sent animals before. Old sheep mostly. Except for Sir fucking Woolston, but he'd been special, like I said before. No, it was the thought of carting our flock of fifty prime and healthy merinos off to slaughter that sat ill in my stomach. And what about our four-year-old sheepdog, Billy, and Banjo? My guts squirmed at the thought of them locked away in a shelter, alone and severed from everything familiar.

I'm not one for praying. I learned long ago at Mum's bedside that it was a waste of time, but that didn't stop me from closing my eyes and fervently hoping what I imagined wouldn't come to pass.

An arm curled around my shoulders. Dad. I blinked, coming back to myself. It was dark, and Banjo was curled up on my lap. When had that happened? Dad pulled me close. To his credit, he didn't make promises or try to give me false hope. He might not have started out as a farmer, but Mum had taught him well. He knew the realities of farm life, just as I did.

"Let's make dinner," he said, instead. A call of agreement issued from the lounge, like the warble of an old magpie. He grimaced. "Preferably before Nan gets the grumps."

That night I dreamed. It was twilight again and I stood among a flock of sheep, heavy wool coats pressing in on every side, my own wool coat thick and hot on my back. A dog barked at our heels and as one we jolted, stumbling forward. A panicked bleat rippled through the flock. *Going. We are going.*

Where? I wanted to ask.

Another bark, and we lurched on again, our hooves sinking into grass and mud first, then clattering up a metal ramp. A truck. The non-sheep part of my brain recognised it for what it was. Metal and death it smelt like. Death, metal and misery.

I locked my legs, but my hooves slid on hay and muck and the flock carried me on and in, packing together tight, and tighter again. My forehoof slipped and I fell to my knees, releasing a panicked bleat. *Stop,* I thought at them, *stop.* But they came on, dozens of them. Feet struck my side, knocked my head. Woolly bodies packing so tight that they couldn't move, and still more came. Tighter and suffocating, until at last it eased.

Under us, an engine hacked to life. Its rumble a roar to our ears.

Between the slats of the truck and knobbly sheep legs, the farm receded. The grass of the paddock pulled away, fences and trees zooming into the distance. Past the barn and shearing shed we went, past the hen house. I watched it all go, until with a wrench, the farmhouse flashed past in a blur of blue weatherboard and tin roof. Away. Away from everything I knew and loved. I opened my mouth, perhaps to scream, maybe to cry, and a long, low bleat came out—

I woke in a tangled mess, sweat soaking my pyjamas, and knew a moment of dislocation. Who was I? Where was I? When? For a heartbeat my head swam before my gaze landed on the desk in the far corner, a school bag slouched over the back of the chair, the patterned rug on the floor and a chest of drawers beside an open window. My room. I breathed out and flopped back to my pillows.

Then vaulted back up again as a long, low bleat drifted in on the wind.

Not part of the dream.

Cold drenched my limbs, rising the hairs on my neck. I scrambled out of bed and ran to the window, pushed the curtain aside.

Sir Woolston was standing in the paddock. *Standing*. Right under the gum Dad had buried him by, clear as day. One look and I knew it was him. I could recognise the curl of those horns anywhere, even if one was broken.

But that wasn't what sent fear clenching through my stomach.

He was looking at me.

I staggered from the window. The ram was dead. I'd seen it, watched Dad bury its mutilated corpse—all twisted limbs and oil marks mixed with bloody wool. Sir Woolston hadn't deserved that end, I'll admit. Not like that. But the ram had definitely died. It wasn't like he'd come off second best with a scooter. He'd been crushed under an eighteen-wheeler cattle truck. It was amazing there had been anything left of him to bury.

I peered back out the window, sure I was imagining him; some subconscious guilt making me see things. A scream sputtered and died in my throat as my airways cinched shut.

Sir Woolston was still there, still looking. But he'd moved. He stood at the edge of our veranda, a faint glow haloing his body. My legs went weak and I gripped the windowsill. I could see *through* him. Right through his middle to the weeds and mottled paving stone under him.

Oh yes, he was dead all right. No thanks to me. But the stubborn git wasn't done. Not yet.

The ram let out another low bleat. A moan almost. Fuck.

I slammed my window shut, drew the curtains and dove for the bed, pulling the covers high over my head. *This can't be happening.* Of all creatures with unfinished business, of course it had to be Sir bloody Woolston who'd come back to haunt me. He was too stubborn to just go quietly. I ground my teeth, fresh rage working a heat up in my belly. Wasn't it enough that he'd tormented me every day while he was alive? And now in death too? My hand clenched into fists. How dare he.

I threw my blankets off, threw open my door and marched downstairs, not sure what I would do until I spied Dad's shotgun by the door. I snatched it up. Too light though—no ammo. I rooted around in the kitchen drawers until I found a round, shoved the shell into the chamber and pumped the slide. That ram would pay for crossing me. I whirled on the door. I would Ghostbusters it out of existence.

"Emma?"

A husky, warble fell over me, freezing me still with my hand on the door. I turned. Nan stood in the hallway, cane in one hand with her other holding onto the doorframe. Her white nighty hung off her like a sack.

"It's all right, Nan. Go back to bed."

Nan snorted and hobbled over, unusually spry for her eighty-eight years. She eyed the gun in my hands, then to my surprise, nodded. "Good," she said. "About time someone did something about that racket."

Her gaze travelled to the lounge-room window and out to the paddock. I stared at her. "You hear it too?"

"How can I not? He's been doing it all bloody night." She shooed a hand to the door. "Go on, silence the fucker. He's dead already, time he got the message."

I gawped. I mean, Nan had always had a mouth on her, but this was something new.

"Would do it myself," Nan went on, "but—" She gestured at her cane. "Do us a favour, eh? So we can all get some shuteye?"

I swallowed. We'd talk about this later, I promised myself, and headed for the door. Nan shuffled after me.

A twist of the knob and I was out on the veranda. Nan stayed there as I padded down the steps and across the damp grass to the edge of the paddock, heart in my mouth, finger on the trigger.

I scanned beyond the fence, waiting for a ghostly set of horns to come charging at me—maybe even *through* me for all I knew. And I'd probably shit myself if he did. I swallowed and took a few steps closer, palms clammy around the shotgun.

Then I lowered it, relief rushing out of me in a long breath.

Sir Woolston was gone.

The veranda lights flicked on, snapping shadows back into the recesses of the deck.

"Emma, what the hell are you doing?" Dad's voice roared from the front door, so loud I yelped and nearly pulled the trigger. I spun, my heart throwing itself into my ribs as if it was trying to break down a door.

It looked bad. I knew it did. "Dad, I—"

He strode forward, fury flushing over his face, and ripped the gun from my hands. In two practiced motions, he had the shell out of the chamber and in his palm. He glared at it, then shoved it before my nose.

"You could have killed someone with this."

Well, that had been the idea. More or less. Perceptive, Dad was, in his way. "There was a . . ." My voice and confidence plummeted under his glare. ". . . noise," I said, switching the word 'ghost' out at the last moment. "Nan heard it too."

"And you thought to investigate with a *gun?*" Dad struggled for composure, deep breaths, clenched jaw. Not good, he was really mad. "With *Nan?* What if she'd wandered off, Em? Or fallen down the steps? Or grabbed for the gun?" He ran a hand through his bed hair. "Christ. You got to think about these things, Emma. *Think.*"

I balked, indignant. "She came on her own. Fully lucid, I'll add. It's not like I bloody kidnapped her." I searched for my cane-totting grandmother to back me up and spotted her at the far end of the veranda having a heated argument with a flowerpot. My insides sank. "Nan?" I asked, going over to her.

"No, I won't fucking tell them. Tell them yourself—well, that's not *my* problem, now is it?" she hissed at the weed-stricken perennials.

I put a hand on Nan's shoulder, gentle-like. She jumped, coming back to herself, and swayed on her cane. "Emma? Oh good, did you shut up that goat yet?"

"It was a ram, Nan," I said, fighting down disappointment. For a moment, just a moment, I'd thought I'd glimpsed the old Nan back in the driver's seat. But no, the disease was at the wheel instead.

My strange and adoring grandmother was losing her mind.

Maybe we both were.

"But did you get rid of it?" Nan insisted as I guided her back into the house and to her room. Dad flashed me a look as we passed, one of those 'I'm not done with you yet' looks that make my insides curdle. "Is it gone? Can I finally get some sleep?"

Truth be told, I wasn't certain on either count. "Yes," I lied as I put her to bed and pulled up the blankets. "Night Nan."

"Night Anna."

Hearing Mum's name leaving her lips nearly broke my heart again.

Sir Woolston came again the following night. I was restless. After finishing my chores, I'd been marched back to my room to "reflect" for the rest of the day (Dad's idea of punishment, seeing as it was a Saturday). Didn't matter that I was sixteen and not six anymore. Not that I minded much, any excuse to avoid Dad's gaze was a welcome one. A master of the old guilt trip was Dad. Just thinking about his last words the night before made me squirm.

"I'm disappointed in you, Emma."

Like I said, I was restless that next night. The full moon was out, if you take stock of that sort of thing. I know I do. Animals go weird on a full moon. Ask any farmer. So perhaps that was why I twisted and tangled in my pyjamas half the night until I heard it again: a long, low bleat.

My eyes popped open. He was back. That was the first thing through my head. Back to finish what was started. I crept to my window, heart banging on my ribs like a judge's gavel. Guilty. Guilty. Guilty.

I chinked the curtain.

Nothing. No glowy woollen ram in the paddock, nothing off the veranda.

Another bleat. Loud and close. He was at the door. My stomach barrelled into my spine as if it might cut its losses and make a run for it.

When no one answered, Sir Woolston snorted and moved. I stood rooted by the window, listening to the *thunk-thunk* of the ram's feet travel the length of the veranda. A windowpane rattled. He was trying to get in. Must be. I imagined Sir Woolston's head pressing against the lounge-room window, angry little eyes peering in. A high-pitched squeaking rose from below: that would be his ghostly horns leaving a laceration across the glass. My belly shrivelled. He was looking for me.

A bleat sounded under my window. My heart shot into my throat, lodging somewhere near my larynx. I wheezed in a breath. Could he get up to the second storey? I slammed my window shut, flicked the latch, and backed away. Better to not find out.

Under my feet in the room below, I heard Nan stir: a creak of bed springs as she got up and her cane clacking on the wooden floor. Muttering, before she bellowed:

"Shut up, you flaming sheep. Fuck off! You hear me? Skat!"

Something cracked against her window. Loud. Too loud to be Sir Woolston. Her cane, probably. Then the tinkle of glass breaking.

Strength drained from my legs. *Oh no. No, no, no.* Cold swept through the floorboards. Below, Nan cried out. I made to scream but the urge for silence seized me, its hands smothering my mouth and commanding me to not even breathe.

Sir Woolston stood before me. In my room. On my rug. Wisps of grey curling off his wool. He was bigger than I remembered, mismatched horns sharper, eyes darker. I scrambled backwards, tripped over my own feet and landed on my arse.

Warmth ran down my leg. Oh shit.

Sir Woolston lowered his head, black eyes fixed on mine.

"No," I begged.

He charged.

I screamed. Or I thought I did. Though I don't remember any sound.

He hit me dead on, right in the middle of my chest; horns to sternum. Horns *into* sternum. I boggled as Sir Woolston's ghost dove into me. Pain seared through my ribs; emptied my lungs. I flew across the room, slamming my head on the foot of the bed.

One last hit, was it? I thought, dimly. Wanted to have the last bloody say? I struggled to my feet, nursing my head. Sir Woolston was gone. "Fucking ram," I muttered, and rubbed my sternum. It smarted something chronic. Probably bruised the bone, if such a thing was possible. I winced and cursed again. Then my fingers ran over something hard. A knot of scar tissue between my breasts, shaped in a rough 'V'.

What the—

A bleat boomed through my skull, as if I'd shoved my head into the flute of a church bell. Light exploded across my vision. The world tilted.

And I knew no more.

I woke to dark and a throbbing in my fingers, like I'd been digging through grit. Cold caked my knees, turned my toes numb. Above the tops of the gum trees, stars shone, a full moon high overhead. Midnight going on morning, to my mind. And my heart lurched. When had I come outside? Cold pushed against my fingers and I looked down. My hands were clawing at the earth, nails cracked and fingers bloody as they tore chunks of soil and rock free.

What the— I made to stand, but my legs wouldn't respond. My hands continued to dig. I tried to pull them away and a growling bleat reverberated in my head, rattled my teeth. Horror shivered through my gut, and I very nearly released my bowels, again.

Sir Woolston.

The ram's ghost was still inside me. It had to be. But what was he doing?

I watched one hand shovel out a fist full of freshly turned soil and deposit it in a pile beside the hole. *Freshly turned soil*, the thought returned, just as my fingers brushed something soft in the earth. Oh sweet shit—

My fingers dusted the dirt off Sir Woolston's corpse. The pungent scent of decaying flesh wafted over me. Ripe to the bone. Dad had only buried it the night before, yet it stank like it'd been the ground a week. The smell gagged in my throat, caught in my nose and I wanted to turn away and puke. But my body wouldn't obey. My hands dug around the woollen limbs, tracing up along the broken spine, dug some more until my fingers touched horn.

The centre of my sternum tingled, and I sensed an eagerness there; a presence leaning my body in, desperate to get my hands around it. I fought the feeling, gritted my teeth and tried to pull myself away. In a flash, my hands clenched around the exposed horn, knuckles white and bloody, and wouldn't budge.

Move, I commanded my legs. *MOVE.* Bit by bit, my knees unlocked, muscles twitched, pulled and lengthened as I stood—still hunched over as Sir Woolston refused to relinquish the grip on his own deceased head.

"Let go!" I grunted. I leaned backwards, fighting the weight of the corpse. Anymore and I'd pull the corpse from the ground like a blood-soaked daisy. My fingers tightened until they burned, and a furious 'baaa' rang in my ears. Bloody prick of a ram. I thrashed, an odd sight it would have been had anyone come upon me, a girl in the dead of night, filthy with grave dirt, and bucking her body as if possessed. Which I was, to my mind.

I was mid-thrash when the neck of the corpse snapped. A pop ran through my arms, as if I'd been bending a stick in two until it gave. One moment resistance, the next none. There was a wet, sucking sound and I pitched backwards, a severed, half-rotted ram's head in my lap.

I screamed—Sir Woolston allowed me that—and tried to fling the thing off, but my hands remained glued to the horn. It dangled in my grip, eye sockets empty from where the critters had gorged; the second horn still snapped mid curl. His nose was gone, a black cavity in its place, as if his face had fallen in on itself—which, I considered, as my heart eased back down my throat, had probably been the case.

But to decompose this fast... I pushed the thought aside as the bile rose in my stomach.

"Now what?" I demanded into the night. If Sir Woolston thought I was taking this rotting skull back inside the house he had another thing coming.

The ram's presence shifted inside me. A cold chill creeping along my bones as he moved away from my hands and down to my legs. Control returned to my fingers and I dropped the head in a heartbeat. It landed with a splat in the grass, rolled sideways once and was still.

Wham! Rage flooded my senses; bellowed in my ears until my head spun. The place where Sir Woolston had hit my sternum smarted. I rocked on the spot, blinking hard to clear my vision, and felt the accursed ram gathering strength—or energy or *something*—to attack again. Bastard was not letting this go.

"All right! All right!" I threw my hands up in surrender—I'm not sure why I did, with him being inside me, but it felt right. I picked up the sheep's head again.

Sir Woolston settled inside me, as much as a cranky old ram can settle. A whisper of cold clenched my fingers tight around a curling horn, as if to say 'keep hold of that', before its presence descended down my legs to force one step, then the next.

"Where are we going?"

A belligerent bleat, short and clipped. Shut up. Righteo then.

We crossed the paddock and for a horrible moment I thought Sir Woolston was headed for the farmhouse, only to veer off course at the last minute and head up the hill. We crossed dewy grass, hay and dead leaves sticking to my bare feet. Up and over fences, across fields, under shadowed gums. I lost track of time. We walked for what felt like hours. I sought out the moon, thinking to find it low in the sky and dawn not far off, only to see it still at its peak.

Time was at a standstill.

A bleat and a burning tingle across my chest roused me out of a stupor. I blinked awake. We stood on the edge of a lush field, too lush for our neck of the woods. A bonfire blazed in the middle of a field and around it hunched figures danced, knock-kneed and stamping. Cold prickled down my legs as Sir Woolston set us moving again. We drew closer, and the chimes of bells seeped into the night, oddly muted, as if I were listening through a closed door. The fire's heat licked over me as we came close, stinging my cold cheeks. And there, at the edge of the gathering, we stopped. The cold in my feet oozed away as Sir Woolston released my legs.

We were here. Wherever here was.

The figures were smaller than me, the tallest barely came up to my chest. But as though to make up for it, their shadows stretched absurdly long in the wake of the fire, two, perhaps even three times bigger than my own (I checked). Their limbs were thin, too. Spindly.

"Where are we?" I demanded. "Who are they?"

Silence for my troubles.

One of the figures detached from the frolicking and approached us, coming closer and closer again, until I could make out its features.

I gawked. A bird might have built a nest in my mouth it was open that long.

They were sheep. Well, not sheep *per se*, not as I knew them with their woolly four-legged bodies and long faces. This was a sheep-*person*. What I'd taken for a hunched back was a cape of unwoven wool around her shoulders. I say her, but I had no way of knowing, her chest was flat, and a woven wool frock covered everything else. The face was long like a sheep's and she had the ears poking through the tight coils of her white hair. A sheep bell tinkled around her neck. The rest of her features appeared human, in a stretched and angular sort of way.

She stopped before us, gold-yellow eyes studying me, and the weight of that gaze bore into me—old and ancient. I shifted, suddenly aware that I was still gripping Sir Woolston's rotting head. I swallowed and imagined how I'd meet my end at the hands of a flock of fairy sheep. What would it be? A lynching? Stoning? A roasting over the fire? Did fairy sheep even eat meat?

Then, to my surprise, she beckoned.

A tingle of anticipation rippled through my chest, then a soft bleat in my ears, almost . . . gentle? Encouraging? I scowled. What was he playing at?

The fairy-sheep girl turned and strode back towards the fire. Five steps in, she stopped and turned to check if I was following.

A faint flush of cold ran across my shoulders, as if Sir Woolston had put a hand to my back and nudged. Then a stronger chill rushed down my legs and into my feet as he prepared to take control again.

"All right, I'm going!" I snapped, exasperated and adjusted my hold on his head and strode into the gathering.

If bleats could purr, Sir Woolston's did then.

"Emma." Warm hands tapped my face. "Emma, wake up."

My eyes opened to blue sky, a smattering of cloud, and Dad's face leaning over mine. Relief flooded his features.

"Thank God," he breathed. His hands fluttered over me. "Can you sit up?"

He helped me sit and I squinted through the morning. I was in the middle of a paddock, under an old familiar gum. Downhill I spotted a familiar broken gate. Sir Woolston's paddock. I rubbed my head. It felt heavy; tight behind my temples, like I had a migraine coming on. My eyes stung.

"What happened?"

"I don't know. When I saw you lying here through the kitchen window, I thought . . ." Dad's voice choked off into a sob; he rubbed his eyes. "God, Em, I thought it was bad. Real bad." My gut knotted, guilt and grief clutching my chest. I knew what he meant. An aneurysm, like Mum. He'd been the one who'd found her, unconscious in one of the back paddocks. Nothing the doctors could do. Her brain was gone. Watching him—*letting* him—turn off her life support was the hardest thing I'd ever done. And he'd thought it was happening all over again. I hugged him, hard.

"I'm okay," I lied and mumbled the only excuse I could think of. "I must have sleepwalked."

We broke apart, a muddy imprint of me left on his shirt. I plucked my filthy pyjama top, sniffed and nearly gagged. It smelled like shit. Literally shit. And probably a hundred other things I didn't want to think about. What had happened last night? Everything was clear—well, clear*ish*—until I stepped up to the fairy sheep's fire. Then nothing but flashes. The fire roaring high. Dancing. Woollen fairies swaying and stamping. My shadow ballooning and stretching across the ground.

I glanced over at Sir Woolston's grave, hoping Dad hadn't yet seen what I'd done to it, and stopped. It was whole. The overturned soil was neatly packed down under the old gum. No sign of my midnight grave robbery. No ram entrails exposed for the crows. Nothing but a quiet mound.

My stomach dropped, a tremble working up from my knees and into my hands. I clenched the hem of my top to stop their shake. Had I imagined it? Had *any* of it been real? I felt giddy. Was I losing it? Cold sweat prickled over my body.

"I need to go have a bath," I heard myself say. I pushed past Dad and stumbled for the fence and the way out of the wretched paddock.

Dad hurried after me. "Are you *sure* you're okay?" he asked.

"I'm fine." I pulled apart two lines of barbed wire and slipped through. The rusted barbs grabbed at my pyjamas, scratching through fabric to skin underneath, then I was clear and marching for the house. My skin felt clammy. My vision tunnelled.

"Em!" Dad called after me, and I heard him swear as the barb wire fence caught him where he tried to squeeze through after me. "Do you want to talk about it?"

It's nothing, you know. Just me losing my mind. No biggie. On second thought, no. Dad had enough on his plate as it was. Nan was enough work already. I all but ran up the steps and through the front door.

"Emma, is that you?" Nan called from the lounge as I blew through. I didn't answer, instead I strode down the hall, into the bathroom, shut the door and turned the shower on as hot as I could stand it. Then I curled into a ball under its stream, clothes and all, and shivered.

It took nearly an hour before the chills subsided. At last, when the heat returned to my fingers, I turned off the shower, peeled free my sodden night garments and towelled myself dry. The tension around my temples hadn't eased, but at least the smell had. Mostly. When I moved, I still caught a faint whiff of smoke. I rolled on extra deodorant for good measure and paused at the sight of my nails.

They were ragged and torn, and despite my soaking, flecks of muck were still trapped deep under each fingernail. Like I really had spent half the night digging. My stomach did a little twist, a flush of adrenaline spiking my veins. Maybe I hadn't imagined it. Hope seeded in that little well of doubt.

I crushed it. Who was I kidding? Possession? Fairy sheep? *Come on, Emma, just listen to yourself.*

Towel wrapped around me, I dug around for a comb to tear out the grass burrs stuck in my hair. "Get a grip," I told myself. I wiped away a streak of condensation from the fogged-up mirror—and nearly screamed.

A ram's skull looked back at me.

My heart cracked into my ribs, and I leapt away. In the mirror, the skull did the same. It wore a blue towel wrapped around its human body. Slow dawning sank in. Swallowing, I took a shaky step forward. So did the skull, bobbing closer on a sunburnt neck and a familiar set of shoulders—one bore a fresh scratch from a barbed wire fence.

Me. It was me.

I lifted one hand and pressed it to my cheek. Smooth skin met my touch, but in the mirror, my fingers met skull.

Explains the headache, part of my brain muttered. I pushed the thought away and studied my reflection. The skull rested on my head like a morbid carnival mask, covering half my face. My human chin jutted out under its nasal cavity; my eyes stared through two hollows. One horn curled down from my temple, almost touching the nape of my neck, before sweeping up again into a tip level with my cheek. The other was snapped mid coil.

My belly knotted. This was Sir Woolston's skull.

It was not the rancid thing I'd dug up last night. No rotting flesh or peeling skin. It was smooth, clean bone, near white but for a blackening of soot around the eye sockets and nose cavity. As if flames had burned away the last of the flesh.

I scrunched my forehead. In the mirror, the eyes behind the skull wrinkled. This was connected to whatever I'd done, or rather, what Sir Woolston had done. Assuming I wasn't batshit mad, of course. Which was likely. But there had to be a logic to it.

So, what the hell had happened last night? What wasn't I remembering?

I sank onto the rim of the bath and closed my eyes. Retrace your steps, that was what Mum had always said whenever I'd lost something. Never thought I'd have to use her advice to track down my own memory. I pictured the last thing I recalled: teetering at the edge of the gathering as the sheep girl with the weight of a millennia in her gaze beckoned me in.

My feet crunched over the grass, the long and unkempt stalks had tickled my aching calves. She'd drawn me to the fire, motioning me to throw something in. A bleat sounded in my ears. Excited, eager. The sensation built, travelling from my chest and down my arm. Sir Woolston nudged my hand, his presence brushing cold around my fingers gripping his head.

I'd frowned. "Why?"

The fairy girl rested a light hand on my arm, guiding it to the flames. "To make right." Then with a long look that make my skin shiver, "You owe him that."

Guilt clenched its gnarly fingers into my gut. "But I didn't mean to..." I began.

The fairy's fingers clenched around my forearm. Her eyes turned hard as faceted amber. "Do it."

Sitting on the bathtub, I ran my fingers down my forearm, bumping over the beginnings of a bruise under the skin. Bastard fairy. I rubbed my temples. What then? I'd thrown Sir Woolston's head in and . . ? My mind's eye served up nothing but more flashes. Sheep bells chiming between the pop and hiss of the fire. The rotting head hitting the flames. And then, more a *feeling* than anything else. A giddying tug at my sternum—Sir Woolston—then a rushing, like I'd released an enormous breath. Then lightness. Freedom. Like I could float away. And euphoria. Somewhere between drunk and dreaming, to my mind.

A knock sounded on the bathroom door, then a husky, "Emma, how much longer will you be? Nanna needs a piss."

I started up from the tub. This could wait. I threw my muddy clothes in the wash basket, adjusted my towel and opened the door. Nan stood in the hall, cane in one hand, a towel and a tea cosy tucked under her other arm. "Sorry Nan. I'm a bit of a mess this morning." My gaze dropped to the tea cosy. "Shall I, uh, get you a fresh shower cap?"

Nan waved me off. "Nothin' wrong with this one." She peered over into the steamy bathroom. "Are you finished?"

"Ah, yes, all yours." I stepped aside.

"Thank you, darling." Nan squeezed past me. "But best take off that hat, you look ridiculous," she said and closed the door.

I waited in the kitchen, listening for the squeak of the bathroom door opening to signal Nan was out. She had seen the skull. Dad hadn't, but she had. I was not crazy. Two people couldn't share the same hallucination, not to my mind. Not when I hadn't primed her or anything.

But I had to be sure.

I stirred my coffee absently with a spoon and took a sip. It was stone cold. I gagged and spat the mouthful back into the cup and put it in the microwave.

"She's near, you know. That's why she sees it," a voice said behind me. A strange voice. One I didn't recognise.

My hand flew around the handle of a saucepan and I whirled. "Who—"

No one was there. The kitchen was empty, so was the entrance hall and lounge beyond. I frowned.

"I've never seen a Speaker in the flesh before." A man in a faded Guns N' Roses shirt and skinny jeans appeared at my shoulder, eyeballing my profile.

I yelped, stumbled back, stepped on the hem of my jeans and landed smack on my arse. Pain smarted through my coccyx. I choked down a howl of agony and whimpered instead.

The man winced. "Sorry, I always forget how finicky Fleshies are about boundaries." I glowered at him through my pain. He appeared late twenties, though it was hard to tell. He had a look of sickness about him. Sunken eyes, hollow cheeks. No hair. Not even eyebrows. And pale. I could see the kitchen benchtop through him.

Another ghost.

My mind garbled out the first thing that came to it. "Fleshies?"

"That's you, the living folk."

What certainty I'd had about my faculties drained away. Why, yes, a small slice of insanity for breakfast, please, thank you. I swallowed. Everyone had their quirks, right? I tightened my grip on the saucepan, for all the good it would probably do. "You going to possess me?" I asked.

"Me? No. I'm not into that." The ghost snorted and waved my concern off with a gesture that reminded me of Nan. I blinked, recognition flicking on a distant memory. I studied his face and saw Dad's eyes and Nan's nose.

"You're Uncle Michael."

The man beamed. "You remember me! I didn't think you would."

"Well, it's more that you look like Dad without hair." I eased the saucepan onto the counter but kept it within easy reach. Along with the salt. That kept off spirits, didn't it? It did in movies. Then something else Michael had said wormed through my shock.

"What's a Speaker?"

"You are." Michael indicated himself. "You talk to the dead."

"I *what?*"

"Talk—"

"I heard you. What I meant was *how?*"

Michael shrugged. "I don't know how it all works. Every Speaker is different, so I'm told. You're actually the first I've met. But *that . . .*" He pointed to my head, and it took me a moment to realise he was pointing at the skull, "that's a sure part of it." He came close again, and a cold prickle ran down my arm and shoulder as he leaned in to examine the sheep's head masking most of my own.

"He's cursed you well and good."

My heart thudded into my throat. "*Cursed?* I'm cursed?"

"All Speakers are, one way or another." He cast me a sly look, eyes roving over the bone mask and the half broken horn curling from my temple. "What on Earth did you do to piss that old ram off so much?

Broke his gate, got him run over. But still, it wasn't like I'd *pushed* him in front of the truck. He'd done that all on his bloody own. And yet . . . I fell silent, mind returning to the fairy gathering, the dancing and the fire; the rush and joy that had coursed through me when I'd thrown Sir Woolston's head on the flames. It hadn't felt malicious. Not even when Sir Woolston had possessed me. Bloody-minded and stubborn, sure, but I'd not sensed any malice, hard as it was to believe. I chewed my lip. But a curse was a curse, and that meant nothing good, to my mind. "How do I get rid of it?" I asked.

Michael pulled a face, wrinkling his nose. "Hell if I know."

Some use you are, I thought, but didn't say. I didn't fancy another possession and midnight frolic in the paddocks, no matter what Michael said he did or didn't do.

A footstep on the veranda outside made me look up. Dad returning from the hen house, a small bucket in one hand.

"Eggs for breakfast," he announced, plunking down the bucket on the counter. Four small eggs lay inside. I winced. Not many of our hens had been laying well recently. Neither of us could work out why. "Let me do it," Dad said when I made to pick up the saucepan again. He set the pan over the flames, drizzled oil into it and cracked two of the eggs in.

"Emma," he began.

I grimaced. *Here it comes.* The heart-to-heart, feelings and stuff all laid out; exposed with their pants down. I love Dad, dearly, but he didn't know when to let a conversation die. It was like talking to a Goddamn boomerang. I shot a glare at Michael, still standing in the middle of the kitchen.

He held up his hands as if I'd turned a gun on him. "Okay, okay, hint taken." He vanished, but I suspected—no *sensed*—he hadn't gone far; I could *feel* him there, like an itch at the edge of my brain.

"I know it's been tough since Mum," Dad went on. "I'm not around as much as I should be. It's hard for me too."

I blinked. I'd braced myself for another "are you okay?" or even a "maybe you should see a doctor", but this was not what I'd expected. It was worse.

"I miss us," Dad said. "We used to talk all the time, you and me. But now we barely talk at all."

"We talk plenty—" I began.

"I don't mean those 'good morning' niceties, I mean the big things. Where's your head at? What are you feeling? What's new in your life? I don't *know* these things anymore, Em. I miss that. I miss knowing you."

My insides squirmed as I stood there listening. I didn't do feelings. Sure I felt them, languished in some, brushed off others, but I didn't *talk* about them. Because some I couldn't put words to. To try was like picking at a scab. Why couldn't he just leave things be?

"I know selling the farm came as a surprise," Dad said, dropping two slices of bread into the toaster. "I never meant for you to find out like that."

"And when was I supposed to find out? When the 'For Sale' sign got nailed to the fence?" Unfair, I knew, but I didn't care. If Dad wanted feelings, I would bloody well give him *feelings*. Angry ones. "This is my home, and you're selling it out from under me. I *know* it's for Nan," I said, cutting him off when he opened his mouth.

He picked at the eggs in the saucepan; they were nowhere near ready. "It's just a house, Em."

Red rag to a bull that was. My fists clenched and hot rage flushed into my cheeks. "It's not just a house. It's everything here. Everything I know and *remember*. And Mum is—" I stopped. A sudden, exhilarating, Goddamn brilliant thought flashed into my head. Mum.

Hope bubbled into my chest, tingling down to my fingers. Mum was *here*. And I could see her.

I barrelled out the kitchen.

"Emma!" Dad shouted after me. I ignored him, breathless as I raced down the hall, out the back door and through the yard. Cold earth numbed my toes as I ran up the hill to the Karri tree and its gravestone.

"Mum!" I cried, coming to a stop under its boughs. I searched the hillside, looking for a pale flicker, a glimpse of movement. She had to be here.

But the leaves were still; the grave silent.

"Mum?" The hope that had been building inside me shattered, shards lodging into my heart and chest. I choked, *feelings* I couldn't name gutting me with a thousand cuts. My lips quivered and I swallowed, fighting down the heat in my throat. Be a turtle, I repeated my old mantra: draw in my soft bits and let the world batter my shell with me safe inside. But it wouldn't work, my mind refused to bend like it had three years ago.

I stared at the grave.

Nothing. Not even the wind.

And then the heat rushed up and out, spilling down my cheeks.

"Why?" I asked, when Michael appeared beside me an hour later. I sat, leaning against the Karri tree, the bumps and ripples of its trunk digging into my back. The heat inside me had gone, leaving me hollow and dry.

Michael sat down beside me. "I'm not sure. Some stay, some don't."

"Then you've never seen her?"

He shook his head. "Never."

I picked up a dry eucalyptus leaf and folded it in my fingers. The leaf bowed and cracked with little splintering sounds. I folded again. *Crack, crack* it went, brittle, dry veins popping.

"What did you mean before?" I asked. "When you first spoke to me."

Michael cocked his head, a see-through frown pulling his brow together.

"About Nan. You said, 'She's close'."

"Oh, that." He stilled and looked up into the Karri's branches, and I had the sense he saw more than just leaves. "Her time is coming. That's why she can see." He waved at my head, then himself, "you know."

A gumnut-sized lump clogged my throat. "Nan is—" I whispered.

"Dying. Something in her brain. She's known for a while. Years actually. I've been telling her she needs to tell you, but she's adamant she won't."

His words seeped in. And I couldn't respond. All I could do was stare at the grass. "Why?"

Michael sighed, a scowl playing over his face. "Says she doesn't want to be a burden."

"A burden? She's not—"

"I tried telling her that. But you know how she is."

Stubborn as a certain bloody ram I once knew. "How long has she known?"

"She found out just after your Mum."

My stomach clenched. I imagined Nan sitting in a doctor's office in her clashing colours, hearing the news for the first time. Alone while the rest of us dealt with our own grief. And then choosing to remain alone.

I'd thought the heat inside me spent, but its warm prickle returned to the back of my mouth. "Oh Nan." *You didn't need to do that. Didn't need to do it at all.* Michael came and sat beside me, his translucent body brushing against my fleshie one with a cold tingle.

"You've been with her all this time?"

Michael nodded, and I thought I saw a silvery sheen in his eyes. "It's hard, you know, to only ever watch." He toyed with a blade of grass, his hands slipping through the stalk as if grasping air. "Not to be seen, heard or felt. But then they start hearing you, and that's even worse, you know? Because for a heartbeat you hope that soon, maybe, just maybe, you might not be alone anymore." He bit his lip and stilled his teasing of the grass. "I'm a terrible son," he muttered, more to himself than me, and I wondered if I'd judged wrong, whether Michael might be even younger than I'd guessed. Dad had never said how old he'd been when he'd died.

The ghost of my uncle met my gaze. "She saw me for the first time three weeks ago, looked right at me. That was when I knew she was near."

Silence parted the air between us, even as my heart quivered in my chest. I swallowed and forced out the question I'd been avoiding. "How long?"

Michael held up his palms. "I'm not a doctor, but she's seeing more and more into the Everywhen. A couple of days, a week maybe."

Less than a week and Nan would be gone. My beautiful, dear, kind, and yes, batshit eccentric, grandmother would leave us—*me*. I tried to imagine the farmhouse without the clack of her cane on the floorboards, or the shuffle of her slippers. No faint snores from the recliner chair in the lounge. No gaudy knitwear or yarn-bombed trees in the spring. My ribs grew tight around my lungs.

It was happening all over again. I clenched my fists and stood. "I won't let it."

Michael blinked. "What?"

I turned down the track, determination in my stride as I headed for home.

I slapped the dusty records on the table in front of Dad. "You need to take Nan to hospital."

Dad frowned over his afternoon coffee and picked up the crumpled file. "What is this?"

It had taken me all day to find it. First waiting until Nan fell asleep so I could go through her things, second to actually think to check the wardrobe. They'd been buried at the back, in an old shoebox.

"Just read it," I said, fidgeting. I couldn't keep my bloody hands still. I shoved them into my pockets and paced. Dad's eyes scanned the first page, then forgot me as they flicked on to the next and the next, taking in the words I'd read earlier. *May experience confusion, disorientation and other dementia-like symptoms.*

The wrinkles on Dad's forehead deepened into crevasses I could have seen from across the room. I waited until he read the line that had stopped me cold. And there it was. A slightly sharper intake of breath and something like fear flashed over his face.

Inoperable.

Dad was still a moment. Then he swallowed. "Where did you get this?" The paper shook in his hands.

"I found it. When I was putting Nan's washing away." A lie, yes, so sue me. Bigger things were at stake. "*Please*, take her to hospital."

Dad glanced back down at the papers.

"Look at the date," I urged. "It's old. They're finding new ways to treat things like this all the time. Sally from school, her mum had bone cancer and they cured her with some new breakthrough or other."

Dad stared at the sheets as if he didn't understand. "She didn't tell me," he whispered. He rubbed his eyes with gritty fingers.

I sat down opposite and squeezed his hands. "Please. Take her."

He squeezed back but didn't move. "I knew it would happen one day, but so soon—"

"Dad," I interrupted. "It's doesn't have to happen, we'll take her to hospital, get some tests. They'll find a way."

He looked at me then, eyes all wet and shiny and sad. Then his arms were around me, hugging me into the smell of sweat and hay and livestock. He kissed my head. "I'll talk to her."

"No! We need—" I writhed out of his hug. "She's not well. Really not well. She needs help."

Dad stared at the papers on the like a man lost at sea watching his ship sail away. First Michael, then Mum and now Nan. Everyone was leaving him too, surely he understood. I waited for a nod, some sign of approval. Instead, he seemed to sink into himself, broad shoulders hunching in. "It's her choice, Em. We can't force her."

"We can!" I nearly screamed it. And for a heartbeat I was struck with the urge to bow my head and charge at him; tackle him to the ground and shake the sense into him. "Why won't you do anything?! You just sit there and take it! Every time! Why won't you fight for her?!"

"Em—"

"Why didn't you fight for Mum?" This time I did scream, and hot tears turned the world into blobs of shape and colour. I drew a ragged breath, the words rise out of me, ugly and unstoppable; bleeding feeling. "You could have. But you didn't. You just nodded your head: 'Yes, Doctor, I understand Doctor.' Nothing you can't do, bullshit. You could have waited. Could have given her more time. That's all Mum needed. Just a little more time. But you turned off the switch."

The Dad-shaped splotch flinched as if I'd slapped him. Another dragged breath. This time from him. I braced for the retort, for the barbs to come flinging back at me. Instead, nothing.

A brush of liquid fingers at my elbow; cold tingled up my arm. I rounded on Michael. "What?!"

"You're out of time."

She lay in bed, a knitted patchwork pulled up to her chin. One arm was exposed; a blood-pressure cuff wrapped above Nan's elbow. Doctor Patel glanced once at the reading, then released the Velcro.

"Keep her comfortable," was all she said.

Dad and I trailed her out to the kitchen. Dad's face still hadn't regained its colour—not in the twenty-four hours since we'd rushed into Nan's room and found her unconscious on the floor. I fiddled with the pull cord of my hoodie, vaguely aware of my fingers knotting and unknotting the string. Invisible beside me, Michael hovered. Literally. Every now and then the light would catch his translucent flesh-or-whatever and he'd flicker in the corner of my eye, like the halo of a migraine, to my mind.

"Quit that," I muttered, rubbing my eyes. My head felt tight, like Sir Woolston's skull was squeezing my brain between his horns; a final 'fuck you' from the dead ram.

Michael shot me a glare. "She's my family too." He drifted over to Dad, and the two of them peered at Doctor Patel in earnest, both of their expressions mirroring one another in that oddly familial way.

The Doctor met Dad's gaze. "How much did the hospital tell you?" she asked.

That her condition was advanced; something about the MRI showing a tumour obstructing her Temporal Lobe—wherever that was—and pressing against her brain stem. And, more to the point, that there was nothing they could do. Dad said as much to Doctor Patel.

She motioned us to the kitchen table. All three of us sat, even Michael; he balanced on the back of one chair like a whisper.

"It's unlikely she'll wake," Patel said. "But if she does, she'll be disorientated, and probably won't be able to speak." She studied Dad and I in turn, her brown eyes serious behind her glasses, face carefully neutral. "It would be kinder for her if it's not drawn out." For a heartbeat, a reflection of my ram's skull flashed in her glasses. Then it was gone as her attention shifted to Dad. "Pray for it to be quick and painless, if that is something you do."

"It isn't," I cut in.

"Emma—" Dad started.

Patel held up a hand. "It's fine." She studied me again, lingering on my face before her expression softened. God, I hated that look. Pity. I'd had my fill of it after Mum. I shoved my chair back and made to stand, but Dad caught my wrist.

"Em, please." His hand slid into mine, squeezing my fingers tight, like he was scared of losing me. It was just the two of us now after all. The thought was like a knife between the ribs. I swallowed hard and sank back to my seat, my grip tightening around Dad's. From his perch, Michael stared at our hands, a quiet longing in his gaze.

"What do we do when—" Dad stopped, dragged in a breath, and his next words came out husky. "You know."

"Call me. I'll take care of it."

He nodded and laboured to his feet to show her out. The moment they stepped out to the veranda I got up and padded back down the hall, back into Nan's room. She was still there, still wrapped up under the covers, a slight fall and rise of her chest that said she was still with us. I turned to the silvery ghost sitting on the edge of the bed, watching herself sleep. She still wore the blue hospital-issue pyjamas and the canary-yellow cardigan I'd slung over her shoulders when we'd brought her home.

"You need to get back in there," I told her, pointing at Nan's body.

Nan's ghost blinked, coming out of her stupor. Her form was faint, like a washed-out watercolour, but growing stronger every time I looked at her. "What was that?" Her eyes narrowed. "I thought I told you to take off that hat."

Instinctively, I reached for my head and cursed Sir Woolston under my breath when my fingers met nothing but hair. "I can't," I said. "You need to go back."

A bubble of hope grew inside me as she seemed to consider it. "No," she said at last. "It's all achy in there. And it smells funny."

Trust Nan put it like that. I tried again. "You can't stay like this. It's not good for you."

Nan snorted and rocked back on the bed, cracking her ghost knuckles. She wasn't as solid as Michael; some part of her still tethered to her flesh and bone perhaps. "Feels bloody brilliant if you ask me." She rounded on Michael beside me. "What's that look for?"

Michael hesitated, sharing a look with me. Apparently, this was a first for him too. "You're dying, Mum."

Nan stilled, silent a long moment. "About goddamn time," she muttered.

"Nan," I began, motioning to her body in the bed. "Please. Go back."

She jutted out her jaw. "You never knew how to let things go." She grimaced. "Got that from me I suspect." Her green eyes turned on me, and for a heartbeat I was reminded of the ancient fairy sheep in the field, old eyes that had seen more than anything had a right to.

But I wasn't about to be lectured by my grandmother with literally one foot in the grave.

"Nan—" I started again.

"No buts," she snapped. "Your tongue is so silver you could mint a year's currency with it. I'm not listening. It's my last day and I'll do as I bloody well like."

I turned to Michael for help. The hint of a smile that had been playing on his face fell away. "You can't force her. Speaker or not."

Of course not, like a curse could never actually be useful. And here I was speaking to the ghosts of my dead uncle and nearly dead grandmother. Like a crazy person. Fuck me. Perhaps I was insane. I ran a hand through my hair. There had to be a way.

Nan jumped up from the bed. "Walk with me," she said, striding to the end of the room in a way I hadn't seen her do in years. When I didn't move to follow, she crooked an eyebrow. "You're going to deny your old Nan her dying wish?"

When she put it like that, I didn't have much choice.

Nan's dying wish turned out to be multiple dying wishes. We headed down the drive, onto the bus and into town. Nan's old bingo hall was empty, but she wandered the hall, drifting between imagined sets of tables. We walked down to the seafront, scattering gulls as we approached. Nan leaned out over the jetty railing and sucked in a breath of sea air—or perhaps it was an imitation of breathing, it wasn't like a ghost had lungs.

"I'll miss this place." She pointed to a rusty lamppost at the shore-end of the jetty. "I kissed your grandfather there, you know? That very spot. Eyed him out at the disco I did, brought him down here."

I cocked my head, suspicious. "And was that all you were doing?"

A grin. More gum than tooth.

"Bloody hell, Nan."

Michael laughed. "You scoundrel."

Nan's grin faded as her gaze landed on her dead son; nearly invisible in the midday glare. "I wished so many times you could have more time to love." She hesitated, then cupped a hand to his cheek. "You were so young."

"I knew love, don't you worry." He looked away and I sensed awkwardness between them. Words left unsaid. "I know you didn't like him, but Will was good to me."

Nan quivered, her whole form rippling like someone had cast a stone into a pond. "I was wrong."

Michael took Nan's hand in his own and held it, staring at their clasped fingers—hers wrinkled and curled, his smooth and young, both of them translucent. Something flickered in his face, an echo of that longing I'd seen before, mixed with relief perhaps, maybe pain. "I thought I couldn't forgive for a long time," he said. "But then I saw what you did for Will. How you'd visit every other day to make sure he was okay. Talked him into finding love again." A small smile. "I saw it all. I found my peace long ago, Mum."

"Then why—" I started and bit my tongue before I could finish the thought aloud. *Why did you stay?* If Mum had moved on, gone into the—what had Michael called it, the Everywhen?—why hadn't he? Unless . . . *Nan* was the reason Michael had stayed here? The thought pulled in my chest. He had stayed when my Mum had moved on, or whatever dead things did. I wanted to ask, but that was his business, to my mind. So I kept my mouth shut, and let mother and son have their moment. When I looked at Nan again, her ghostly form seemed stronger somehow, more defined. More like Michael. The lump grew warm in my throat and I left them on the jetty, the pair of them looking out to sea like two clouds who might blow away in the wind.

The bus ride back to the farm was a blur. We walked up the driveway—cutting through Sir Woolston's paddock didn't feel right— and when the farmhouse came into sight, tin roof all lit up orange in the sunset, my throat closed. Not yet. I detoured Nan to the barn. She'd always liked animals.

Banjo greeted me at the door with a rasping mewl and rubbed his face against my leg. When Nan crouched to greet him, the tom hissed and bristled as if he might swipe. I pulled my leg away from the crossfire.

"Can he see you?" I asked Michael.

"I don't think so. But he feels us. A lot of animals do."

He was right about that. The horses stamped and nickered to each other when we passed their stalls, and Billy the sheepdog ducked into his kennel at our approach. Even the chickens stayed on the far side of their coop.

"I'm sorry, Nan," I said, expecting some sort of upset, perhaps even frustration. Instead, she wrapped a hand around my own, her touch sinking through my skin and chilling my fingers numb.

"They understand," she said. "I'm not supposed to be here."

My stomach knotted. *No, not yet.* The skull squeezed my temples, as if it disagreed.

Nan tapped my arm. "It's time."

"Where have you been?" Dad demanded the moment I walked through the door. He looked distraught, hair dishevelled, his five o'clock shadow well on its way to bristle, bags under his eyes. Neither one of us had slept last night—I probably looked much the same come to think of it.

I'd had it in my mind to tell him about his mother and brother's ghosts padding off down the hall—he had a right to know after all, they were his family too. But when I opened my mouth I chickened out. "I . . . needed some air." I shoved my hands in my pockets. I should have brought flowers or something. Then, before I knew what was going on, Dad was drawing me into a hug, smoothing my hair.

"I'm sorry, you're here now. That's what matters."

I took a breath; the sweaty, unwashed scent of his shirt filling my nostrils. My stomach cramped. I had to tell him. This was Dad. If I had to tell anyone, it should be him. I swallowed. "Dad, I . . ." Again I hesitated, not sure how to put it all into words; Sir Woolston's curse, Michael's haunting, Nan's spirit growing more solid every minute. "I think it's soon," I said. *Fucking chicken.*

His hug tightened, and he kissed the top of my head. "I know."

"Michael's with her."

Dad paused, cocking his head. "I didn't think you remembered him."

"I've become . . . reacquainted."

"You know, I never said anything to Nan as I didn't want to upset her, but every now and then, I get the sense that he's near." He hesitated, a slight tension running through him arms as he held me. "Sometimes your Mum too."

I stiffened and heard the barely audible intake of Dad's breath. *And I never said anything to you, as I didn't want to upset you either.* The words hung unspoken between us. I forced myself to relax; not to let the hope rush up inside me. The skull on my head tightened, the weight of its horns straining my neck, as if Sir Woolston was back in my head, berating me. I bit back a scowl, forced down the disappointment again. Mum was gone, I knew that.

"I'm okay," I said, and winced at the lie. "I mean, I'll be okay." I scuffed a shoe. "I'm sorry, about what I said yesterday."

Dad did what Dad did best, he waited. He was good like that. Patient. He never pushed. I'd always figured it had been from working with animals for so long. Maybe it was, maybe it wasn't.

"I know you fought for Mum, in your own way," I said. And it was true. He'd been the one after all who'd found her, rushed her to emergency, clung to her side every minute of every test until the doctors were sure. All I'd been able to do was stare. I hadn't even been able to bring myself to take Mum's hand. I'd just stood and watched, wishing I'd wake up. I'd hated myself for that.

"I wish I could have been like you then," I admitted and felt my throat warm. Fuck I hated feelings, but this needed to be said. "Nan was right. I'm shit at letting things go." I wanted to fight for Mum, for Nan, but sometimes to fight for someone was to know when to stop. Nan had shown me that. It had just taken a while to sink in. "She told me she's ready." I swallowed a gob of spit and unshed tears and went on before my voice broke. "I'm ready now."

Dad held out his hand. "Let's go."

I nodded and took it.

Nan's breath was faint; her eyes still under her eyelids, a halo of grey curls around her head. Dad and I sat on vigil, hunched in kitchen chairs pulled up on either side of her bed. Together we watched the rise and fall of her chest, each time thinking, this one would be the last.

And still Nan stayed.

Her ghost sat at the end of the bed again. She was almost solid, the bedframe barely visible through her. Next to her, Michael appeared dull and milky as he held her hand. I cocked my head at him, confused. She'd said it was time, so why was she still here?

He shrugged, helpless. "I don't know."

When I caught ghost-Nan's eye, she glared back.

"Don't ask me. Hell if I know."

I rubbed my neck, trying to ease the tension from the skull. It had grown heavier in these last hours, pulling the muscles tight in my neck and pressing around my brow. It was everything I could do not to rest my head on the covers of the bed and close my eyes for a moment's respite. I shifted and massaged my forehead. Wretched curse. When I died, I would give that ram a bloody piece of my mind, or better yet, a boot up the arse for buggering off to the Everywhen and leaving me with a skull trying to squeeze my brain out my ears.

"You okay?" Dad asked.

"Just a headache," I said. Partly true.

"I'll get an Aspirin," he said, rising.

"No, it's fine." I caught his wrist. "Stay, you don't know when . . ." I trailed off and glanced at Nan. Truth was, I didn't want to be alone when it happened. Not with her ghost right here watching. It didn't seem right to my mind. None of it did, come to think of it. I opened my mouth to say something, anything, and stopped.

Dad was staring at the end of the bed. At Nan. "Mum?" he said. His eyes flicked to the ghost beside her, his lips parting. "Michael?" He went still, as if scared he might frighten his brother away.

Nan's ghost rocked to her feet, her eyes alive.

Michael's head snapped up.

Dad gaped. "You're . . ." his voice wobbled, and he stepped towards them, pulling my grip free of his arm. Then he blinked, looking around the room, confused. "Where did they . . ?"

It couldn't be. I reached out, touched him again, this time on the elbow. Skin to skin. Dad sucked in a breath and his eyes darted from Nan's body under the covers then to her ghost at the foot of the bed. He swallowed, eyes misting. "This is it, isn't it?"

Nan leaned close, pecked a kiss on Dad's cheek. "Not forever," she said. "But until then, yes, this is goodbye." She grinned at him, more gum and teeth, then kissed his other cheek. "Thank you, my boy."

Michael came forward and Dad ogled at him, unable to get any words out. For a moment, I worried Dad might faint. I shouldn't have. This was Dad, he took it all in stride, even as the tears spilled out of him and he choked out something unintelligible.

"I know," Michael said, and hesitated, then clasped Dad's shoulder. "I'll take good care of her. I promise."

And, like that, something in my head gave—a loosening in my neck. A stitch unravelling around my temples; an easing in my lungs, like a breath releasing. My skin prickled, hot and cold flushing through me—the same as that night at the bonfire with Sir Woolston's ghost. Behind, there was a low, finale sigh from the body in the bed. Before us, Nan's ghost shimmered; her glow fading.

I released Dad's arm. "She's gone."

He nodded, mute. Staring at the bed.

Beside me, the two ghosts hovered. One freshly minted, the other old and well-past his time here on Earth.

"Where to now?" Nan asked.

A soft bleat called in my ears. I shivered, the way becoming suddenly clear; pulling in my chest the same way a pigeon always knows true north. I held out one hand to Nan and the other to Michael. "I know a place."

I found my way easily enough. When I stepped into Sir Woolston's paddock, felt wet grass under my feet, the land just *shifted*. I walked, the world twisting itself around me in a blur of trees and hills and sky, until I arrived to where I needed to be. Had I not had two ghosts in tow, I don't think I could have done it.

The field was exactly as it had been. But the figures around the bonfire had changed. They'd thrown off their sheep skins, wearing loincloths of hide and fabric instead. They stood taller, lankier than before, horns gone and hair long; their forms mirroring the human spirits before them. All that said, their eyes remained the same, gold and ancient beyond reason. Perhaps that was the way of things here—them shifting to match the dead who found their way here. Maybe it was a comfort thing. Or reassurance.

Nan, Michael and I stood before the fire, its heat buffeting my hair and flaring our shadows long behind us.

"You're sure about this?" Michael asked.

I shrugged. "It's where Sir Woolston went, and he seemed pretty happy about it." I recalled the rush, the freedom roaring in my bones, and was halfway tempted to step into the flames myself. But no, this was for ghosts like Nan and Michael. I might be a Speaker to them, but I wasn't one of them, not yet anyway. Truth be told, I wasn't quite sure what I was.

Michael and Nan exchanged a glance. "We're ready."

"Then jump," I said.

They didn't. Instead, Nan reached for me, cupping my cheek, just as she had with Michael on the jetty half a world away. "Thank you." She wagged a finger at me. "And whatever you do, don't let your Dad sell the farm."

I blinked. With everything else I'd clean forgotten about the sale. Not that we needed to worry about that now. The thought sucker punched the reality home. This was it. I clamped my jaw, in part to gulp the heat of a sob down and partly to stop anything silly from spilling out. I nodded instead.

"Good girl." She took Michael's hand. "Ready?" she asked.

"Ready."

Together, they leapt into the flames. Their woops rang in my ears, and I felt them go; their departure a sudden lightness in my body, like a part of me was drifting up into the smoke with them. I wiped my eyes with a sleeve. *Bastard ram,* I thought, turning for the trees and back the way I'd come. The ancient figures danced around me, their shadows twitching under my feet, and my shadow mingled into one with theirs.

Sir Woolston sure had pulled one last doozy on me. Michael reckoned it was a curse. But I think he was wrong. It was something, but not that. Perhaps a gift, in Sir Woolston's twisted way. A final "got you" from one stubborn git to another.

With a sigh, I stepped back into Sir Woolston's paddock, the world settling into a familiar rusted fence and paint-peeled farmhouse.

Bloody ram always did get me in the end. One way or another.

About the Author:

Nikky grew up as a barefoot 90s child in Perth, Western Australia, before moving to New Zealand in 2016. By day she works as a professional content writer and by night authors speculative fiction, often burning the candle at both ends to explore fantastic worlds, mine asteroids and meet wizards. Her creative work has appeared in magazines, on radio and in anthologies around the world. She is currently writing a dark fantasy trilogy, routinely sacrificing literary darlings to the editing gods in the hopes of seeing it published.

You can find her online at:
W:nikkythewriter.com | T:@NikkyMLee | F:nikkythewriter

THE ATONEMENT OF ARIES

Rohsaan McInnes

And down then from the rocks comes the fire, flaming red and dark.

The hero, the magic man, it calls with a roar, no longer a bleat,

On its back it carries humanity's scourge,

The powerless, the infirm, and the empty and bleak.

With superhuman power it walks above the earth, unseen.

In the stark space of the wide alone,

Where the heat of no being lingers,

The hero, the magic man, must atone.

In its heart, it suffers the wrongs it must keep, hidden from light,

Alone, it rests, curled horns and wool, a horizontal stare,

To take the burden with no reward,

It can't forget, it aches, it has seen, darkest despair.

But he is just a man.

Also, of naked skin, and toes and hands, a human soul,

Red and deep, he bleeds, his mind drifts in the wrongs,

Wounded. No peace. It is that which they stole.

Curled horns and wool, a horizontal stare, it bleats, it roars.

Ready to be a hero, to save one, or many, to save them all,

And over again, deep down, a thousand burdens he hides,

It is the fate of Aries, the magic man, forever to suffer and fall.

About the Author:

Rohsaan McInnes grew up in Geelong, in south eastern Australia, and graduated from the University of New England in 2005 with a Bachelor degree in languages, linguistics and literature. She writes mostly young adult fiction because she digs it, and she also happens to live with 4 young adults who help her to remain cool. Rohsaan's first YA fantasy novel, The Quadrants, is published on Amazon and we are expecting #2 in the trilogy any day now.

Rohsaan is also an artist who spends part of each year painting. Specialising in semi-abstract portraits, she is planning to finish a collection this year with the aim of exhibiting. She also takes commissions and even entered the Archibald Prize for the first time in 2019.

You can find her on Facebook and Instagram.

THIS IS THE DAWNING (PART IV)

Helena McAuley

Night had swallowed the world by the time Capricorn and Doug made it to Bicentennial Park. They'd covered the three blocks from Pisces' house at a run, and Doug bent over, bracing himself against his knees and drinking in the cool air. Of course he had struggled to keep up with Capricorn; Doug only had a meagre, human form.

"What now?" he asked between gasps.

Bicentennial Park was large enough to have its own circuit track, but small enough to exist amidst the suburbs. A man-made recreation of wilderness; hills and dales, paths crisscrossing it, groves of rocks and trees surrounding an artificial lake.

Capricorn's eyes scanned the park. "This way," he murmured, and ran again.

Doug staggered after him.

There had been no more metaphysical screams since they'd left Pisces' home, but even Doug had sensed a tension in the night air. Fear and terror that were not his own pulsated in the back of his brain. Once he'd filtered out the burning pain and overwhelming noise the mental communication caused, he'd been able to hear the voice clearly—feel it, clearly. Capricorn had said it was one of their own, but it sounded like a young girl. Doug's stomach clenched in anxiety.

Capricorn led him into an artfully designed grove, and they knew they were on the right track when they saw a large backpack discarded among the trees, its contents spilling across the moss and lichen.

"Oh no," Doug breathed. It was branded with the logo of the local secondary college.

A scream splintered the calm of the night—an actual scream this time, not one of the mind. They ran towards it, fear pushing Doug to ignore the building acid in his muscles. They spilled down a small slope into a cutaway, and he saw her.

She was maybe fifteen or sixteen years old, fallen to the dirt and abutted against a decorative boulder. Dark hair, dark skin, dark eyes wide in terror.

And standing above her fallen form was a goddess. *Of course,* Doug reasoned. The antagonist is always beautiful. She appeared only a few years older than him, tall and lithe, auburn hair streaked with grey, eyes of blazing turquoise. She had one perfect hand raised above the girl as if to strike.

Capricorn bellowed into the night. "Sagittarius!" He thrust one hand before him, and a beam of yellow light shot from his palm. It struck Sagittarius in the chest and she was thrown into the trees.

Doug recoiled in shock. "Woah!"

"Look after the girl," Capricorn ordered, and disappeared. He'd unmanifest; at least Doug was able to take *that* in his stride.

He slid down the slope into the clearing and crawled over to the sobbing girl. "It's okay, it's okay," he cooed. "What's your name?"

She swallowed hard and replied in a small voice. "Mia."

Doug smiled at her. "Okay, Mia, we're gonna get you out of here. Can you stand?"

"I think so . . ." She huddled into him and together they hobbled from the clearing; she grimaced in pain at every step. "I think I've sprained my ankle."

"It's okay." He braced her with his arm, and she drew closer. "Just take your time." They didn't bother to retrieve her schoolbag, and as they burst from the trees into the open night Doug looked up and saw a starlit sky with only wisps of clouds. Among the clouds two lights danced and flickered—one of yellow, and one of burning red.

"Oh my!" Mia gasped. "Is that a UFO?"

Doug opened his mouth to correct her, then hesitated. "Sure," he said instead. He half pulled, half carried Mia through the park, glancing constantly at the lights flashing in the sky.

Their path led them toward the lake, before they would have to attempt the hilly terrain back up to civilisation and safety. At least, he hoped civilisation equated to safety. He really didn't know the rules about this stuff.

Mia stumbled, gasping as she tumbled to the ground. Doug was instantly kneeling at her side.

"My ankle," she moaned, tears standing in her eyes. "I don't think I can make it."

"Hey, it's okay," he assured her again. "You can do this. You seem pretty tough to me."

A look came to her eyes, at once pleased by the compliment and embarrassed by it.

Uh oh, Doug realised. *She thinks I'm flirting with her!* Oooo, this wasn't good. She had to be at least five years his junior and slight enough to be mistaken for younger again. His thoughts were less complimentary. *Yeah, dude. You're going to jail.*

Doug glanced up as the red light flew across the sky and barrelled into the yellow, which flickered and fell. The yellow light careened towards the earth, growing brighter as a burning corona engulfed it, before the silhouette of a falling man could be seen. It crashed into the ground, leaving Capricorn's broken visage.

Mia screamed.

"Cap!" Doug shouted and ran to him. "Cap! Speak to me!"

Capricorn stood, unharmed, and affixed Doug with a stern glare.

"I told you to get her out of here!" he hissed.

Doug looked back over his shoulder. Mia still sat in the grass, her dark skin pallid and muscles frozen in alarm at the sight of the indestructible man. Her chest was heaving, eyes so wide that Doug could see all the sclera. Suddenly, her head snapped back with a sickening gurgle and her body tensed, every muscle utterly rigid and immobilised, her breath caught in her throat.

"Mia!" Doug called.

Capricorn let out a breath. "Here we go."

Mia screamed; a piercing cry of torment and agony. A pale nimbus encompassed her, the glow hovering over her skin, before it penetrated her, bright light spilling from her eyes and mouth to cut a swath through the night. The scream reached its crescendo, and her hair became streaked with grey.

"Mia?" Doug squeaked.

Sagittarius appeared, hovering in midair as she looked down at them. "Aries."

"You took your goddamned time!" Mia snarled.

"You didn't have to wait for me before you incarnated," Sagittarius quipped.

The smile that lit Aries' face was full of dark mirth, but devoid of humour. "Yeah, I know. But it's more fun with you." She launched herself from the ground and struck Doug full in the chest. The force took his breath. He couldn't even scream as they tumbled down the hill, one atop the other.

"Aries!" Sagittarius shouted.

Capricorn turned to move, but Sagittarius lashed out and the bolt of red light caught him in the shoulder.

Doug and Aries continued to tumble, the ground striking a new part of his body with each bounce, until he collided with the soft grass at the bottom of the dale. Aries landed in a crouch on top of him and grasped a handful of his shirt, dragging his face towards hers.

"So, Aquarius, you think your time has finally come?" Her voice dripped with sweet darkness. "Well, I guess it has."

"But I'm not—!"

Her small fist rendered the rest of his sentence moot, as it did his nose. She grasped him with both hands, rolling from him and throwing him into the air.

Doug felt himself turn, and landed with a crash that stole what breath he'd recovered from his lungs. God, she was strong! His chest burned and for a moment his lungs refused to inflate. He turned and Aries stood over him, her hand raised towards him.

Capricorn appeared beside her and wrenched her arm away; the crimson bolt flew into the night sky.

She spun and smacked Capricorn in the mouth with enough force to snap his head back. She jumped and latched on to him, bringing her fist down into his face three times in brutal succession.

Capricorn pressed both hands to Aries' chest and the resulting blast of yellow light sent her flying into the air. She used her momentum to turn the fall into a flip and landed in a crouch.

Sagittarius was suddenly before her. "Let's go."

"Hades that," Aries growled. "Kill them now. Two less to deal with later."

"Sagittarius!" Capricorn shouted. "I know you killed Gemini!"

She turned on him, and the nearby trees suddenly cascaded with fire. "You're a fool, Capricorn!"

"Do not pursue this, Sagittarius," Capricorn said, his voice was heavy with warning and threat. "The proper order must be followed."

"*Your* order!" Aries spat. "*Your* precious plan! You would have broken the order to see my Age denied!"

"Your Age nearly sent the world into destruction!"

"My Age was a time of growth!" Aries shouted, throwing herself at him, but Sagittarius held her firm. "The fire burns away the chaff and reveals the wheat! Consumes the trees so the forest can thrive! I am a necessary element!"

Capricorn's eyes narrowed. "But not a desired one."

"I am desire!" Aries roared.

Sagittarius grasped her shoulder. "Not now." Aries made to push past her, and Sagittarius' grip tightened. "Trust me," she hissed.

Aries looked up at the taller woman, her face set with burning anger. But she relented. Her eyes turned to Capricorn.

"I'll look for you in battle."

The two women took to the sky and were gone in an instant, the twin lights of bright red and crimson fading into the distance. The conflagration of the trees died to embers, then to smouldering ash, leaving the gums as bare trunks bereft of leaves.

Doug rolled onto his back and stared up at the wisps of cloud and stars. His breath had returned, but his ribs still hurt like hell.

Capricorn entered his vision, staring down at him—stern and hostile. He seemed to be about to speak, but only turned his head and released a frustrated breath. "From now on, you do not leave my sight. Not until this is finished."

Doug nodded from his prone position. It was all he could manage.

Capricorn sank into the grass beside him, resting his elbows on his knees, and released another frustrated breath into the night.

In the ensuing silence Doug filled his aching chest with air, feeling the pull on every muscle and the cold left in the pit of his stomach from his waning adrenaline. "I think my ribs are broken," he wheezed. "And maybe my nose."

Capricorn glanced briefly at him. "Nothing's broken."

"I'm sorry we lost Aries," Doug said.

"It's Aries," Capricorn replied. "There wasn't much we could do."

"I'm sorry I'm such a rubbish battle partner."

Capricorn watched Doug, assessing him. "What melancholia have you fallen into that you need this continual reassurance?"

Doug remained resolute in mute embarrassment.

Capricorn looked away. "I didn't bring you because I thought you would be useful," he told him. "I brought you because I hoped battle would trigger you to incarnate."

"Like it did with Mia?"

"Who? Oh." Capricorn nodded. "Yes, as it did with Aries."

Doug's hands were interlaced over his stomach as he lay in the grass. He nervously began pulling at his fingers, twisting the digits around each other in awkward patterns as he kept his eyes affixed on the sky. The pain in his chest was steadily lessening, confirming Capricorn's assertion that his ribs were not broken. "They're very different, aren't they?" he asked quietly. "Aries and Mia."

Capricorn seemed distracted. "I wouldn't know," he muttered. "Five minutes isn't really enough time to get to 'know' a human."

Doug hesitated. "You said I wouldn't change," he breathed. "If I were to incarnate. But Mia did. She was a really sweet girl, but then she became a Queen Bitch Goddess."

"I never said you wouldn't change," Capricorn corrected him. "How could you not? You're simultaneously being exposed to all your past incarnations, as well as your true nature and the world of the spirit opening to your mind. Of course you would change, but you would also remain who you are."

Doug focused his eyes on the blades of grass, towards the trees, and away from Capricorn. "It looks like it hurts," he muttered.

Capricorn only hummed an assertion.

"Capricorn"—Doug's voice was barely enough to break the night—"do you even like me?"

Even turned away he could feel rather than see the snap of Capricorn's head as his gaze fell on him, could know the indecisive assessment in his eyes, the formulation of which words to say, and which words to keep silent. That alone spoke volumes to Doug. Capricorn's answer was not forthcoming, and Doug immediately understood; it was because Cap didn't know the answer himself. He had not taken the time to consider the question before it was asked, but now that it was, it brought to stark light all his glaring faults. Just a human man-boy. With each passing moment Doug retreated further into himself. His embarrassment and shame building like a bleak cocoon, as was the desire for that cocoon to swallow him whole.

"Mere hours are not enough time to know a human, either," Capricorn finally replied.

Doug pressed his lips into a thin line, his fingers and toes curling in on themselves. He kept his gaze firmly away from the demigod. So that answered that, then.

"I wouldn't make a very good ruler of an Age," Doug said. "I can barely keep my own life in order, never mind being responsible for the fate of all humanity. I'm pretty much the embodiment of one big screw-up."

Again, the response was not immediate. And again, Doug sank deeper into shame.

"That is a very *human* way of thinking," Capricorn said. He stretched his legs out on the grass with a groan and rested back on his elbows, his head tilted back up to the sky. "Pisces is the ruler of this Age," he said towards the stars. "In these last two thousand years, she has been incarnate sixteen times. And to each incarnation she has only given a human lifespan." He paused to allow the knowledge to sink in. "As with most of our fellows, she has spent more of this Age dis-incarnate than incarnate."

"Has she always been a massive hippy?" Doug muttered, bitterly.

"*She* has not always been a woman."

It was this statement, more than the knowledge of Pisces' limited incarnations, that spoke to Doug. He glanced back to see Capricorn, his face unreadable, and slowly sat.

"An incarnation is an expression," Capricorn continued. "You are who you are, just as Pisces is what she is, because of a desire to express something; a desire to feel certain emotions, to live certain experiences, or accomplish certain goals. I guess"—he scratched at the stubble on his chin—"even as we are guarding and guiding you towards becoming more like us, we are trying to learn more about what it means to be you.

"You don't need to *be* anything, *do* anything, in order to be the ruler of your Age," he explained. "What you represent, what you *are*, will permeate every fibre of the physical world. This Age of Aquarius is the culmination of our work. Just as the Arian Age was a time of conflict and yet material growth, and this Pisceran Age has been an Age of the coming together of the spiritual and the material, a 'death of the gods', if you will. The Aquarian Age will unite all these dangling threads into one coherent form. It is Aries' nature to focus on what is before her, it is Pisces' to live with half her mind among the clouds. It is *your* nature to see the spiritual *in the* material, so the two are one, no longer separate, but unified. It is what is required for humanity to finally grow beyond their physical limitations."

Doug remained silent. This was a lot to take in. He was just 'Doug'; nothing special, no master guru. Heck, he wasn't even sure if he believed in a spiritual realm. So far he had accepted everything Capricorn had laid before him, even if it had taken him a couple of moments. Fantasy novels, comic books, video games, and a desire for something more had created the fertile ground his mind had needed to readily embrace the journey. But he had given no thought to the destination. "How many times has Aquarius been incarnate in this Age?" he asked.

"Twice, including yourself."

Doug fell silent. Twice? To Pisces' sixteen? Pisces had said that incarnation was not their natural state, but surely there was some kind of attraction to the physical realm that kept them coming back. An attraction to the experience, to the *expression.* Then what was it that Aquarius didn't want to experience? What was he hiding from?

Finally, he asked, "Has Aquarius ever been the ruler of an Age before?"

"Yes. Many times."

Doug felt his stomach turn cold. "And how did they end?"

"In chaos," Capricorn told him. "As all others have done. That is why I implemented this plan."

Doug's leg was jittering on the spot, a nervous habit he'd developed as a child. There was a question burning on the edges of his thoughts, but he was unable to capture and inspect it. He took a breath and opened his mouth, waiting for the question to spew out. "If the Aquarian Age is supposed to be a paragon of peace and prosperity," he said cautiously, "Why does it have to begin in war?"

"Not war," Capricorn said. "Consensus. Those of the Twelve left incarnate need only agree." He shrugged. "Of course, that is not always possible."

Doug's lips tightened. It was a sorry state of affairs. All to propel humanity towards an evolution it may not be ready for . . .

Though it had been proven many times that Capricorn was not a man the age he appeared, he still groaned like an old man as he stood.

"You need food, you need liquid, and you need sleep," Capricorn said. "Pisces has agreed that we can stay at her home. Come on, we'll continue in the morning."

Doug rubbed at his face, regretting the action and wincing at the tender bruising and dried blood. "All right," he said. He stood, and the two walked deeper into the night.

After an icepack and some antiseptic cream, a quinoa salad, and another cup of that disgusting tea, Douglas fell asleep on the couch without prompting.

Pisces and I excuse ourselves into the kitchen and let him sleep. With any luck, it will be the last sleep he'll ever need.

"Aries incarnated as a what?"

"A child," I tell her. "She's just a little girl."

Pisces shakes her head and wraps her arms about herself. "So typically Aries," she tsks. "Acting without thinking. Always leaving things till the last minute."

"She tried to strike him with an emanation," I add. That statement silences her for a moment.

"Aries tried to emanate Doug? But he's still human!" She shakes her head again, her disapproval evident. "That's just bad form."

"Aries was never going to side with us. If I'd known who was calling, I would have just ignored it."

"Oh, Cap." Pisces dismisses me and crosses to the sink to refill the kettle. "You were always too hard on Aries."

I hold my tongue on that comment. There's no need to re-walk dead ground. I lean back against the bench and change the topic instead. "Who have you been able to speak with?"

Pisces sighs and looks up at the ceiling. "Virgo and Cancer vowed allegiance for Aquarius," she said. "Although Cancer wouldn't say anything direct, so I'm not sure if the vow can be trusted."

"And Virgo would simply side with whomever asked first," I add bitterly. "What about Leo?"

"Refused to answer the question. Wasn't too kind about it, either."

I admit, I smile. Leo's sheer arrogance would have made that an entertaining conversation.

Pisces moves to rinsing the teacups. "I couldn't locate Taurus or Libra."

"I know where Libra is. I'll take care of it."

"Is that a good idea? You and Libra—"

"We're fine. I'll take care of it. Did you manage to contact Scorpio?"

The washcloth stills in Pisces' hand, the kitchen silent except for the running of the water and the snap of the switch as the kettle boils.

She turns to me with pleading eyes, lips pressed and pale, stretched thin. I nod my comprehension; she's too scared to speak with Scorpio. I can understand that, too.

"Never mind," I say quietly.

"You know I would," she beseeches. "It's only that . . ."

"It's fine, I understand. You don't need to."

Visible relief washes over her. "Cup of tea?" she asks, her brightness returning. "I have rooibos, peppermint, or rosehip."

"No, thank you. I'd better get back to work." Not least of all so I can avoid her horrible tea collection. I stand from the bench.

There is alarm in her eyes. "You're not going to go to Scorpio now, are you?"

"No. Scorpio can keep." I unmanifest, but she can still hear my words. "It's about time I found Taurus."

To be continued in the next edition of the Zodiac Series—*Taurus* . . .

About the Author:

As a child, Helena McAuley was told that everyone only has so many words for their lifetime, and if you use them up, they're gone. She dutifully pondered this in silence for a moment, then launched into a rant about how it couldn't be possible.
No one has been able to shut her up ever since.
'This is the Dawning' is a serialised debut that will be published throughout the ASF Zodiac series. So if you want more Doug and Cap, you'll have to check out the rest of the series.
She can be found twit-ing, insta-ing, and occasionally facebooked under the handle @thathmc
Public Service Announcement: If you get rammed by a Ram, the best thing to do is go and sheep it off. (Or so I've herd)

ABOUT AUSSIE SPECULATIVE FICTION

Aussie Speculative Fiction is a recently established group which was created to support and promote Australian speculative fiction writers.

Check out our links:

www.facebook.com/Aussiespeculativefiction/

www.twitter.com/aussiefiction

www.aussiespeculativefiction.com

www.books2read.com/rl/asf

ABOUT DEADSET PRESS

Deadset Press is the publishing imprint of Aussie Speculative Fiction—a community aimed at supporting Australian and Kiwi authors. You can learn more at:

www.aussiespeculativefiction.com

ALSO BY DEADSET PRESS

Annual Anthologies

Beginnings: Aussie Speculative Fiction Anthology Vol. 1

Journeys: Aussie Speculative Fiction Anthology Vol. 2

Drowned Earth

Prequel: Shards of Silver by Alanah Andrews

The Rise by Sue-Ellen Pashley

Fire Over Troubled Water by Nick Marone

Submerged City by Austin P. Sheehan

Tides of War by Marcus Turner

The Jindabyne Secret by Jo Hart

River of Diamonds by S. M. Isaac

Salvaged by C.A. Clark

Emoto's Promise by Shel Calopa

The Zodiac Series

Capricorn (The Zodiac Series #1)

Aquarius (The Zodiac Series #2)

Pisces (The Zodiac Series #3)

Aries (The Zodiac Series #4)

Taurus (The Zodiac Series #5)

Gemini (The Zodiac Series #6)

Cancer (The Zodiac Series #7)

Leo (The Zodiac Series #8)

Virgo (The Zodiac Series #9)

Libra (The Zodiac Series #10)

Scorpio (The Zodiac Series #11)

Sagittarius (The Zodiac Series #12)